"I hope you're planning to finish what you're starting,"

Gabriel said, as his hand snaked around Joanna's waist and pulled her against him.

There was no need for him to explain what he meant. That knowledge brought her to her senses.

"I'm s-sorry," she stammered, as she tried to step away from him. "Really, Langston, I shouldn't have done that." She looked up, expecting to have him scowling down at her. His brilliant smile was a total surprise. "I'm saying no," she said more forcefully.

"I know, I heard you."

"Then why are you smiling? And why won't you let me go?"

"Because," he murmured as his hand slid up in an achingly slow motion until his fingers entwined in her braid. Gently he tugged until her head fell backward. "This is the first time you've given me any response. I'm just glad to know I haven't totally lost my touch."

"Am I supposed to swoon at your feet, Langston?" Joanna teased.

"Not yet," he said, as he lowered his mouth to hers.

Dear Reader,

I hope you enjoy *The Silent Groom,* my chance to reunite Rose and her family from the earlier Rose Tattoos. Joanna Boudreaux has her work cut out for her when she agrees to defend Rose on murder charges. This job isn't made much easier by the constant presence of the mysterious Gabe Langston. As always, the tension between these two strong-willed characters makes for some fun and lively scenes. Having Rose smack-dab in the middle of things only makes it worse.

While this is a story about past secrets, it is also a chance for me to let you get to know Rose a little better. I always like to think of Rose as an eccentric relative. She can be infuriating, brash, annoying, yet somehow, her kind heart always seems to rise to the surface. I also thought this would be a nice opportunity to let you know how some of the past heroes and heroines are faring. Thank you for all of your kind letters and E-mails asking me "Whatever happed to...?" I couldn't answer all of those what ifs, but I tried to give you a sense of where these people have gone since you last visited them. Please feel free to contact me at http://wwcomet.net/writers/kelsey or through the Harlequin Website at: http://www.romance.net.

1997 will be a year full of Rose Tattoos, with a release in August as well. And I have a few more ideas in the works, so I hope you'll continue your very flattering support of Rose, Shelby and the whole gang for a dose of danger and desire at The Rose Tattoo.

All the best—and happy reading!

Kelsey Roberts

Kelsey Roberts
The Silent Groom

Harlequin Books

TORONTO • NEW YORK • LONDON
AMSTERDAM • PARIS • SYDNEY • HAMBURG
STOCKHOLM • ATHENS • TOKYO • MILAN
MADRID • WARSAW • BUDAPEST • AUCKLAND

For Bonnie Crisalli, who always gave me support: You'll be missed. And for Huntley Fitzpatrick, who is about to learn the meaning of the expression "high-maintenance."

ISBN 0-373-22412-5

THE SILENT GROOM

Copyright © 1997 by Rhonda Harding Pollero

Drawing by Linda Harding Shaw

CAST OF CHARACTERS

Joanna Boudreaux—A very organized attorney. Her defense of Rose could cost her her life...or at least her heart.

Gabriel Langston—His secret might cost him Joanna's love and put Rose in prison for life.

Rose Porter—Her future is in the hands of total strangers.

Don Harris—Is he prosecuting Rose for the murder of her ex-husband, or is his true target Joanna?

Susan Taylor—The star witness for the prosecution, she can place Rose at the scene of the crime.

Lucy McGuire—A chameleonlike bartender.

Dylan Tanner—He knows the case against Rose is nearly airtight.

Michelle Danforth—She's rich, she's beautiful, but is she deadly?

Shelia Porter—She claims she and Joe Don had the perfect marriage, but did they?

Prologue

"I cannot believe that you actually hired the first attorney you found in the phone book," Shelby groaned as she placed her hand on Rose's slumped shoulder.

"She wasn't the first—I made it all the way to the Bs."

Her friend and business partner attempted a smile, though a night in jail had dulled her expression. Shelby, along with everyone else at the Rose Tattoo, was terribly worried. In almost four years she had never seen Rose Porter so upset.

Rose patted the rather lopsided mass of her hair with a nervous hand. "I won't have J.D. shelling out any more money on my account," she announced, her ferocious pride hanging on each word. "Having to call my son to wire the bail money is about all the charity I can stand."

Shelby moved over behind the Rose Tattoo bar and poured two mugs of fresh coffee. Through the mirror behind the neatly aligned bottles of liquor, she could see Rose tilt her head back and close her eyes.

"I'm sure you can meet this woman tomorrow," Shelby suggested as she returned to the table. "By then I'll have enough time to finish filling Gabriel in on what's happened."

Rose's green eyes flew open, then narrowed. "I thought I said I didn't want you to do that. I can't afford to pay Mr. Langston, too. I'll bet private detectives are expensive as hell."

Shelby shrugged. "Rose, we *want* to do this. Dylan can't personally help you," she explained. "And Gabe has been nothing but gracious and friendly ever since he moved in across the street. Besides, he spends so much time here, he's probably desperate for the work. He doesn't seem to have any clients yet."

"How am I supposed to pay Langston *and* an attorney?" Rose fairly shouted, strain evident in her tense features. "I still haven't finished paying off my loan to Mitch Fallon."

Shelby reached across the smooth surface of the table and covered Rose's hand with her own. She felt a small tremor. "Don't worry about the money, Rose. Your future is more important than money."

"But I didn't do it. When the police and that jackass of a prosecutor finally figure that out, I'll be buried beneath so much debt I'll probably have to sell my interest in this place."

"We need to focus on getting you out of this. We'll worry about the money later."

Rose snorted. "That's easy for you to say—you aren't the one writing the checks."

"But I would," Shelby said quietly. "You were there for me when Chad was kidnapped. I asked Gabe to help you. I'll make sure he's paid for his services."

"I don't like charity," Rose warned, her chin thrust out proudly. "I'm already in debt to my son for a hundred thousand, and I have to give this lawyer woman a check when she gets here."

"Maybe you should just talk to her first," Shelby said. "See if you think she's the right one to defend you. I've never heard of Joanna Boudreaux. I still think you ought to take J.D.'s suggestion and hire someone with—"

"I have already heard this from both my sons," Rose interrupted. "I'm sure she'll do just fine. Why should I pay some high-priced name, when I'm innocent? Nothing but a foolish waste of money," she concluded as she kneaded her neck and shoulders. "Money I don't have."

"You know Wesley and J.D. will do anything for you, Rose. And neither of them would expect repayment."

Rose sat forward and leveled her eyes on Shelby. "How can I ask them for help when the State of South Carolina claims I just murdered their father?"

Chapter One

Joanna Boudreaux cursed the morning traffic as she circled the block for the third time. "Think you can make the turn into the alley this time?" she chided herself, slowing as the Rose Tattoo came into view.

"I should have told Mrs. Porter to meet me at my office," she grumbled as she steered her car through the narrow alley adjacent to the historic building. She pulled up and parked between a minivan and a Mercedes. Hoping the Mercedes belonged to her potential client, Joanna felt her spirits lift a little.

Reaching behind her seat, she lugged her overstuffed, well-worn leather briefcase out of the car, shut the door and pressed the small button on her key chain that chirped as it activated the car alarm.

She stood for a minute, taking in the buildings, knowing full well this was the murder scene. That was the main reason she had agreed to meet the Porter woman here. It would save her a trip later. Joanna liked that idea. She was very regimented with her time management, so much so that as she took her first step, the electronic appointment book in her purse began to ding as a reminder that she had this meeting.

Knocking on the door marked Employees Only, she shifted her heavy briefcase to the opposite hand and made a mental note to make an entry in her appointment book to sort through the case that evening. She was fairly certain she had a block of free time between five and seven.

The door opened and Joanna found herself staring at a chest. Not any chest, but a broad male chest in a tight-fitting turtleneck sweater that left very little to her imagination. In spite of the unusually cool April temperatures, she felt suddenly warm as her eyes moved upward. And upward, until she was forced to tilt her head in order to find his eyes. They were an astonishing color—neither green nor brown, yet *hazel* seemed too ordinary a word to describe the golden starbursts surrounding the black pupils. His eyes reminded her of a predatory cat.

His hair, she noted, was pulled back in a trendy ponytail. The hair wasn't the only thing trendy about this large man, either. A round diamond stud glistened in his left earlobe, and it wasn't a chip. Nope. She immediately wondered how a restaurant worker could afford a diamond that size. *He probably isn't claiming all his tips,* she thought with a smug smile.

"You must be Joanna," he said.

His voice was so deep, so incredibly sexy, that she

made another mental note for her electronic organizer: *Get a date with someone—anyone—and soon.*

"I'm *Ms.* Boudreaux," she said in her courtroom tone. "I'm here to see Mrs. Porter."

She expected him to move, but he didn't. Instead he allowed his head to dip to the side as his eyes roamed over her face, then continued down, until he had even made an examination of her slightly scuffed black pumps.

"Look, Sparky," she said with a sigh. "Those bedroom eyes and that oooh-baby once-over probably work wonders when you're tending bar, or whatever it is you do here. But I find it condescending and childish, so please move so that I can get to work."

He didn't even have the courtesy to look properly chastised. In fact, he smiled in a lazy, sensual way that somehow managed to get her to notice the incredible dimples on either side of his mouth.

"Right this way," he said as he moved, but only fractionally.

Joanna sucked in her breath, turned sideways and tried to get past him without making any physical contact. It didn't work. For one split second, she felt the hardness of his well-muscled body against her back. For several seconds afterward, she tingled from the contact.

She found herself in a long, narrow, galleylike kitchen that smelled faintly of grease and lemon. The sound of Elvis Presley singing something wafted from the direction of metal doors with circular windows.

She noted stairs to her left. *That must be where it happened,* she thought, theorizing from what little information she currently had.

"They're waiting for you in there," he said.

Joanna wanted to ask who "they" were. She didn't defend people by committee. The last thing she wanted was a group of friends and relatives telling her how to plan her defense or, worse yet, asking what they should say to best help the accused.

The metal door was cool to the touch as she reached out and gave a small shove. The minute the door opened, she forced herself to swallow her groan. No fewer than five people sat at one of the tables near a horseshoe-shaped bar. The only man in the group stood as soon as she entered the room.

"I'm Joanna Boudreaux," she said, stopping just short of joining the group. "I'm here to see Rose Porter."

The dark-haired man didn't react to her abrupt tone, but the women did.

"I'm Shelby Tanner," said a brunette, who looked as if she had to have been Miss America for at least one year. "Gabe thought it would be a good idea if you had an opportunity to speak to all of us."

"Gabe was mistaken," she said, directing her remark to the man who had risen when she entered. "Sorry, Gabe, but Mrs. Porter and I need to meet in private before I make a decision about taking the case."

"You'll take it," a voice said from just behind her.

Refusing to turn and face the guy who had let her in, she simply sighed loudly and said, "Contrary to what your employee has decided, I'm the one who makes the decision. Now, which one of you is Mrs. Porter?"

Joanna watched as the assembled group exchanged looks, and she had a definite feeling of being the only one not privy to the secret handshake.

Shelby stood then, taking the arm of the woman next to her in the process. Joanna guessed she was about to be introduced to Rose. If so, Rose needed a lot of work before she entered a court of law. It was amazing that the fashion police hadn't arrested her right along with the Charleston PD. If the tight Lycra pants weren't bad enough, the leopard print sweater and gaudy lion's head pin with its obviously fake ruby eyes certainly were.

"I'm Rose," she said in a clear, though tired, voice. "And he isn't my employee. I guess he's yours."

Joanna felt her eyes grow wide as she turned to look up at the smug, arrogant and amazingly handsome face. "Who *are* you?"

"Gabriel Langston," he said as he offered her his large hand. "My friends call me 'Gabe.'"

"Well, *Mr.* Langston," Joanna began as she met his gaze. "I don't need another employee, thanks all the same. Unless you can type a hundred words a minute," she added with an exaggerated stroke of her chin.

"This isn't negotiable," he said firmly, though the sparkle of amusement never left his piercing eyes. "I won't be working for you—I'll be working *with* you."

"I don't work *with* people."

"You do now."

"I HAVEN'T SAID I would represent her yet," Joanna said even before Gabe had ducked beneath the yellow crime-scene tape across the door marked Office. "Thanks to you, I haven't even had an opportunity to conduct a proper interview."

He moved with a grace that seemed at odds with his size. Joanna found that annoying. Basically, she was hunting for a flaw, any flaw. No man should be *that* attractive, *that* self-assured. He must have some hidden, but huge, imperfections. Maybe he left the toilet seat up or the top off the toothpaste. Maybe he was the real killer.

"Who are you?" she asked again. His response to her initial inquiry had been to all but drag her from the room.

"I'm a private detective. My office is just across the street, next to the orphanage," he said, tossing his dark head in that general direction.

Joanna managed to tear her eyes away from him and was suddenly distracted by her surroundings. The room contained two desks, one near a huge bay window, the other against the wall, which was splattered with reddish brown splotches she assumed were blood.

Despite this, she found her eyes returning to Gabriel. Though she was trying not to notice him, she was failing miserably. Gabe went over to the desk by the window, sat down and laced his fingers before sliding them between the chair back and his head. Of course this position made his biceps bulge against the black turtleneck sweater. And of course his dark eyelashes fluttered at just the right moment, giving new definition to the expression "bedroom eyes." Suddenly warm, Joanna stripped off her jacket.

"Nice blouse," Gabe said in an almost mocking tone.

She was standing at an angle to him, so she had to turn slightly to face him. Leveling her eyes on him, she said, "What's wrong with my blouse?" Joanna couldn't restrain the annoyance in her voice. This was one of her best silk blouses. And here she was getting nonverbal criticism from a man dressed like some sort of B-movie cat burglar.

"Nothing…except for the fact that you've still got the dry-cleaning receipt pinned to the tag. I know because it's hanging out the back."

Grinning from ear to ear, Gabe rose, reached her in two strides and placed his warm, large hands on her shoulders. He turned her slightly, but not until their eyes had locked for the merest of seconds. She felt him lift the few strands of her hair out of the way. As if his sexy look hadn't been enough to set her pulse racing, the feel of his slightly calloused fingers exploring the sensitive skin at the back of her neck actually caused her to shiver.

"Cold?"

"Yes," she lied as she grabbed her jacket. It might be her best blouse, but it was also sheer as the dickens, and she wasn't about to let him see the effect he had on her. *Deprivation,* she reasoned mentally. *It's just been too long since my last date.*

"Penny for your thoughts," Gabe teased.

She looked to see that he had returned to the desk by the window, and now sat with his feet propped up on one corner. "I'm still paying off my student loans," she replied, trying to match his superior smile. "I don't sell anything for a penny these days."

Gabe's face suddenly grew solemn. "It happened here."

Feigning shock at the same time she wondered why she was so hell-bent on antagonizing him, she asked, "Really? And what was your first clue? The blood splattered all over the place? Or maybe it was the chalk and tape outline of the deceased?"

She had definitely hit a nerve, and it wasn't a pretty sight. His eyes grew dark, except for the shimmering specks' golden highlight. The gold was the only thing that kept them from looking like the eyes of a shark about to move in for the kill. His expression was so hard, so furious that Joanna made another note for her organizer: *Don't push Langston too far.*

"Look," she began in a more placating tone. "I

don't usually work with detectives. My clients can't afford them and quite frankly, neither can I. I'll bet your hourly rate is more than mine, so this really is a waste of your—''

"I'm doing this as a favor to Rose and Shelby. Money doesn't enter into it."

She didn't bother to hide her grin. "If money doesn't matter, then you must have a lot of it."

Inclining his head as if conceding the point, he said, "As we say in New York, I'm comfortable."

His smile could have charmed the scales off a fish. God, this man had everything—looks, money, intelligence. She felt her shoulders slump. There has to be something wrong with him. Then it hit her—*married.* He had to be married. Joanna only encountered losers, as if she had some big magnet on her back that only enticed the worst of the worst.

The last guy she went out with had seemed normal on the surface. They had shared a nice dinner, then he invited her back to his place—to meet his "Mommy," whom he still lived with at the age of forty-two and whom, it seemed, came as part of the package. The guy before that had taken her to dinner, then passed her the check when it arrived, explaining that working regular hours, holding a regular job, paying taxes and such were all part of a secret government plot to move the country toward Communism and he, personally, was doing his part to rebel. And those were only her most recent encounters. Joanna had such a long history of somehow picking the dregs of the dating pool. It didn't seem probable that a man

like Gabe Langston could just happen into her life. She wasn't that lucky. *Nope, if he isn't married, he probably is the real killer.*

"Were you in your office when Mr. Porter was murdered?" she asked as she moved to the credenza and leaned against it to take some of the pressure off her toes. Damn the person, doubtless male, who had invented the pointed-toed pump.

Gabe shook his head. "Sorry to disappoint you, Jo, but I was—" he hesitated, then grinned and finished "—otherwise occupied."

The grin left no doubt in her mind about what "occupied" was really a euphemism for. "Don't call me 'Jo.'"

"Why?"

"Because."

"Why?"

Exasperated, Joanna sighed and said, "Because my father was the only person who ever called me 'Jo' and he passed away this year."

Gabe nodded and stroked the stubble covering his cheeks and chin. It wasn't stubble from not shaving; it was the intentional kind, the sexy kind. Joanna rolled her eyes and wondered why she was having so much trouble staying focused.

"Well, Jo," Gabe began, unimpressed by her request, "we have our work cut out for us."

"I haven't spoken to Rose. I don't even know if I want the case."

"You want it," he said with supreme arrogance.

The Flaw. *Finally,* she thought with some relief.

"You can't afford to say no to a paying customer, and Rose will pay. Because of where and how Joe Don was found, this case should hit the papers. It's your chance to make a name for yourself."

She resented the fact that he obviously knew more about her than she knew about him. "Maybe I don't want my name in the papers."

"So—" He sighed the single syllable as he rose slowly. "You expect me to believe that a woman who graduated fifth in her class from Georgetown Law is happy doing court-assigned defense work when the public defender's office is overloaded? Or do you get some sort of perverse pleasure out of facing your former boss in the courtroom? You know Don Harris will be prosecuting this himself. I'd think you'd take the case just so you could prove to Harris that he was wrong to have—"

"If I take the case it won't be about Don Harris," she broke in. "How do you know all this?"

"I told you—I'm pretty good at what I do," he answered. "Shelby wasn't too thrilled when Rose insisted on picking you out of the phone book."

So that was how she'd gotten called in. She'd wondered. "I'll have to phone Southern Bell and let them know my ad is working," Joanna returned sweetly. Gabe came around the desk and stood in front of her, literally toe-to-toe. She hated the fact that she had to tilt her head in order to make eye contact with the man. Her traitorous hormones didn't seem to mind his closeness, especially when she got her first whiff of his cologne—expensive and subtle. The "expensive'' part suited him, but ''subtle'' wasn't an adjective she would ever apply to this man.

''We need to set some ground rules,'' he said.

''Okay. I'm in charge and you'll investigate whatever leads I think need investigating.''

He made a sound that indicated he had other plans. ''We're a team, Jo. No secrets, and you are definitely not to do anything that is even remotely dangerous.''

''Dangerous?''

''One of the people you'll interview is the real killer. You'll take me with you wherever you go.''

She felt heat on her cheeks. ''This isn't about dangerous situations. You're my baby-sitter now? Does Shelby think I'm so inept that she wants you to tag along so that I don't screw up?''

''That's her plan. *My* plan is to keep you safe.''

He wasn't touching her, not in the physical sense, but his words did. ''Why do you have this thing about my safety? You don't even know me.''

One dark brow arched playfully. ''Hopefully we can rectify that as the investigation progresses.''

Joanna gave him a light shove backward. ''Be serious, Langston. I'm the lawyer. I'm never in danger, except maybe in domestic cases.''

''But this time you'll be doing the investigation my way.''

She gaped at him. ''I only do things one way. *My way.*''

He shrugged his broad shoulders. ''Then I'll be happy to go down and tell Rose you aren't suitable to handle her case.''

"And I'll tell her I'm perfect for the job."

"But I have Dylan and Shelby on my side."

Joanna balled her hands at her sides, feeling the twinge of pain as her nails dug into the flesh of her palms. For a fleeting second she wondered if it was Shelby who had occupied him last night. Then, remembering the looks and touches between the Tanners, Joanna dismissed that thought completely. True love if she'd ever seen it. "What *exactly* is your way?"

"Just that we share everything and you don't take any unnecessary chances."

"Unnecessary chances? What? Like filing a motion with a typo in it?"

"No, like getting too close to the murderer."

"You seem to be forgetting something," she reminded him in a somewhat softer tone.

"What?"

"Rose might be the real killer."

"Dylan and Shelby have both told me that isn't even a remote possibility."

Joanna moved forward and placed her hand on his hard forearm. "I got the police report this morning."

"Good. We can go over it and—"

"They didn't just arrest Rose because she was Joe Don's ex-wife."

Langston went still, his eyes fixed on her face.

"She was seen leaving here less than five minutes before the first patrol car arrived. Mr. Porter's body was still warm."

Chapter Two

Joanna's organizer chirped at the same instant she pushed through the front door of the Rose Tattoo. Her groan was audible and drew an instant response from Langston, who was lounging against the bar with Shelby's husband, Dylan, and two other men. All held mugs of coffee and it almost looked as if she'd interrupted one of those twelve-step meetings. Tall, burly, attractive men who all seemed as if they belonged in beer commercials and pink plastic stirrers somehow didn't fit in the same picture. Then there was the woman—at least she thought it was a woman—behind the bar.

"This was supposed to be a private meeting," Joanna said between clenched teeth. Though she saw her client seated at a table with four other women, she threw her annoyed words at Langston.

He shrugged without even the slightest hint of remorse. The action caused the smooth rayon of his shirt to billow out from his broad shoulders. The fabric was a pale green that seemed to enhance features that needed no enhancement. Even though she could have happily strangled him at that moment, she also seemed helpless to control her curiosity.

"You're beeping," Langston said. He sauntered over and took her briefcase from her hand, and in those few seconds when his breath washed over her face and his knuckles brushed hers, Joanna felt a warmth begin to surge through her body.

Closing her eyes briefly, she steadied herself and said, "It's my organizer," as she reached into her purse and pressed the button to silence the sound.

"We made these arrangements last night and you were afraid you'd forget in the span of fourteen hours?" he teased.

Joanna stiffened. "No," she insisted as she met his eyes. "It helps me keep track of meetings for the purposes of billing." Of course, she failed to mention that she also stored such important things as when to buy panty hose and when to schedule an eyebrow waxing, but she wasn't about to tell him that.

"I thought we agreed that I needed to spend some time alone with Rose," she said in a whisper as she followed him toward the other side of the room.

"After reading the police report, I thought it would be a good idea if we did everyone at once."

"Except," Joanna began, her temper rising along with her voice, "privacy ensures that one person's statement isn't influenced by another's."

"Which is why I've set up a small interview area on the side porch over there." He paused and pointed to a pair of beveled-glass doors. "It's a little warm, but it's sunny and kinda relaxed out there."

"We aren't doing therapy here, Langston. I don't care if they are warm and relaxed. I only care that I get their statements down accurately."

He stopped and wrapped his square-tipped fingers around her upper arm. "If people feel relaxed and informal, they tend to be more forthcoming and open."

"And I suppose you're an expert on interrogation? Was that included as part of your mail-order certificate to get your PI's license?"

"No." His eyes turned to gold ice as he spoke. "I learned that during my twelve years as a New York City police detective."

Bested. That was the word that came to mind as she watched him carry her briefcase out to the "interview area." His ebony ponytail swayed in perfect rhythm with his trim hips. The silver clip at the base of his head was carved with a plain, masculine design that even ultraconservative Joanna found sexy. Briefly, she looked down at her navy blue suit, white blouse, navy hose and navy pumps and felt about as boring and frumpy as humanly possible. She belonged in one of those women's fashion magazines, with a big black bar across her face under the heading "Fashion Don'ts." She comforted herself with the knowledge that at least her French braid was straight. Then, glancing back over her shoulder, she looked at the person behind the bar and didn't feel quite so bad about her own appearance. Not when she was standing in the same room as someone with a ring through her nose that was connected to her earring.

"So who are all these people?" Joanna asked Langston as she pulled a blank legal pad from her briefcase. "I only saw one name listed on the police report as a possible witness."

"Rose's family is here. The incredible-looking blonde—"

"Is Destiny Talbott," Joanna finished. "I've seen her on television."

"She's married to Wesley Porter, the guy at the bar with the glasses. You know Shelby and Dylan. Then there's Tory, J.D.'s wife. She's the very pregnant one sitting next to Rose at the table."

"And the other woman sitting with them?"

"Susan Taylor. She works here as a waitress and—"

"She's the one who saw Rose leaving just before they discovered the body," Joanna finished. "It isn't such a great idea for the two of them to be chatting together," she said. "If the DA hears about this and Susan wavers even a hairsbreadth from her original story, he'll probably accuse me of tampering."

Langston offered her a reassuring smile, complete with dimples. "Forget Harris for now," he said. "Besides, Rose and Susan are really tight. The only way Harris could keep them apart is if he took Susan into custody as a material witness. After five minutes with her, I'm sure he'd change his mind."

"Why?" Joanna asked as she watched the woman, who had hair dyed a vibrant shade of maroon, as she carried on an animated conversation with Tory.

"Susan is a bit on the strange side."

"Worse than that…person behind the bar?"

Langston's laughter was deep and rich, and had an instant effect on her pulse.

"That's Lucy McGuire. I understand today is punk day."

"Meaning?"

"Apparently she's an actress, or wants to be. Shelby told me she has several personas. Apparently in the short time she's worked here she's become a favorite attraction for the customers."

"But why is she here today?"

"She and Susan share an apartment. I thought you might want to question her after you spoke to Susan."

"And the rich-looking guy at the bar?" she asked, curious about the last unidentified person.

"J. D. Porter, Rose's eldest son."

Joanna thought she detected a slight catch in Langston's voice, but it was no longer apparent as he continued to speak.

"And he is loaded. He's the one who wired the money to bail Rose out after her arrest."

"I'm going to need a scorecard," Joanna mumbled as she dug out her favorite pen.

"You actually have a sense of humor?" Langston taunted, feigning great surprise. "Does your pocket organizer allow for a spontaneous remark? Shouldn't you have waited for another one of those beeps before saying something funny?''

''You're right.'' Joanna sighed. ''Cute remarks are only scheduled for the third Wednesday of the month. I take it back.'' After arranging her pad and a small, voice-activated recorder on the table, Joanna groped in her bag until she found the batteries she had purchased on her way over. She was conscious of the fact that Langston was watching her every move, and it made her irritable.

When she turned the recorder over to pop the battery casing, Langston let out a small grunt. ''What?'' she asked, meeting his gaze.

''Ten bucks says those batteries aren't dead.''

Joanna felt her cheeks flame. ''I don't want to run the risk of having the tape recorder die in the middle of the interview.''

He threw his head back and laughed. ''God, you are anal.''

''And you're annoying,'' she said defensively. ''If you don't like the way I do things, why don't you spare us both a lot of aggravation and quit?''

''You'd like that,'' he said, his expression suddenly serious.

''Immensely,'' she answered.

Just as she was about to insert the new batteries, Langston reached out and placed his hand over hers. His large palm completely engulfed her small hand as well as a considerable portion of the machine. It wasn't the size that bothered her so much; it was the unsettling mixture of heat and strength in his touch that caused her breath to catch in her throat.

"I'm not going away, Jo," he said in a velvety tone. "So you are just going to have to lighten up and admit that you like me."

His arrogance worked like a bucket of ice water. "I don't like you, Langston."

"Yes, you do," he countered.

She could hear the smile in his tone, so she lowered her eyes and counted silently, praying for patience.

"Admit it, Jo. You like me."

"I don't make a habit of lying," she said, glad that her tone sounded even and confident, which was amazing, given the fact that his thumb had begun to make small circles on the flesh at the sensitive underside of her wrist.

"Don Harris would take exception to that."

Joanna whipped up her head and leveled her eyes on him. "The district attorney has nothing to do with this, and I would appreciate it if you would stop mentioning his name every opportunity you have."

He kept his hand over hers, but his thumb stilled. "If you can't stand hearing his name, how do you intend to face him in the courtroom?"

Joanna didn't hesitate as she answered. "As you pointed out, Langston, I graduated fifth in my class from Georgetown. I can handle Harris in the courtroom."

He inclined his head fractionally. "Then all that stuff about you violating—"

"That topic is not open to discussion," Joanna interrupted as she made a futile attempt to pull her hand free. "Let go."

The shake of his head was almost playful, and it went a long way in stoking the fires of her simmering anger.

"Not yet. Not until you admit that you like me."

"This is childish and stupid," she told him on an exasperated rush of breath. "Why do you give a flying hoot if I like you or not? We're stuck together for the time being. We don't have to like each other."

"I like you."

"Great, at the end of the trial I'll make a motion to the court that you be listed as Mr. Congeniality for the record."

"*They* all like me," he said as he indicated the group inside the restaurant.

Joanna sighed again, her annoyance building. "With so many friends, my opinion of you shouldn't matter."

"But it does," he said in a softer, more reasonable tone that managed to chisel away at her anger.

"I don't know why."

"Because partners have to trust each other. It only stands to reason that you'd have to like me in order to trust me."

"We aren't partners," Joanna assured him. "We're…casual professional associates forced together by circumstance. Why are we having this pointless discussion?"

"I'm concerned that you'll allow your personal feelings for me to impair your judgment."

"First of all," Joanna fairly screamed, "I don't have any personal feelings for you. Second, I *never* allow anything to compromise my judgment."

One dark eyebrow arched. "Is that what happened with Harris?"

"That's it," Joanna announced, jerking her hand with enough force to free it from his grasp. Her tape recorder went skidding across the table, then landed on the wooden floor with a terrible-sounding crash. "Great, now look at what you've done."

Bending down, Joanna reached for the miraculously intact recorder and was surprised to feel his hands on her shoulders, guiding her upright.

"I'm sorry," he said against her ear.

"Good for you."

"Joanna?" he asked as he gently spun her so that they stood close together, his fingers wrapped around her arms. "Look," he began in a contrite tone. "I think I went about this in the wrong way."

She glared up at him. "What was your first clue?"

She watched the frustration play with his handsome features.

"Can we start over?"

"Start what?"

He seemed to be fighting a smile. "Our casual professional association," he answered in a mockery of her own words.

Joanna was pretty sure that wasn't the first answer

that had come to his mind, but it did show a small
concession on his part. She didn't answer immediately. Having an investigator, especially one she
didn't have to pay, might be an advantage. But then
again, that was assuming that Rose was innocent, a
possibility that her experience in the criminal justice
system told her was highly unlikely. The police had
had good reason to arrest Rose and there was nothing
she'd read in the report to indicate that this was anything more than a crime of passion, with Rose as the
criminal.

As if reading her thoughts, Langston said, "She
didn't do it."

Stepping out of his reach, Joanna said, "I'd like to
hear that from her."

He seemed genuinely relieved as he strode off to
fetch Rose. Joanna was glad to discover that her recorder still worked, though it now bore a crease of
white paint, which she scraped off with the tip of her
fingernail.

She watched through the opened beveled-glass
doors as Langston walked—no, she amended men-
tally—swaggered into the restaurant, over to where
Rose and the other women were gathered. After
Langston said something she couldn't quite make out,
Rose stood, as did the two men seated at the bar.

They were quite a sight as they moved toward her.
Rose's obviously bleached hair made her stand out
among the dark-haired men. Joanna felt her own
brows draw together as she studied each of the men

in turn. Except for the fact that Langston was slightly taller and broader in the shoulders, he could have been a member of the Porter family. She groaned inwardly at the mere thought. "God, what if Langston is a cousin or something?" she whispered. Rose's immediate family seemed quite protective enough, without any additions to their number.

As soon as the three men and Rose stepped through the doors and into the sunlight, Joanna forgot any musings of a family connection. Wesley and J.D. had the same blue eyes, Rose's were green, but none were like the incredibly unique color of Langston's soul-searing eyes.

Joanna didn't waste any time. "I need to speak to Rose alone."

"Nice to meet you, too," one of the men said without sarcasm as he extended his hand. "I'm Wesley. This is my brother, J.D.," he continued with a disarmingly warm smile.

Joanna shook each man's hand in turn. Langston had moved to stand against the railing and seemed to be studying Rose's adult children intently. Maybe he had some reason to be suspicious of the brothers. Joanna shot Langston a glance, but whatever he was thinking was hidden by a perfect poker face.

"I'm sure you can understand that I have to speak privately with your mother."

Both men nodded and it was J.D. who spoke this time. Reaching into the pocket of his slacks, he unfolded a check and handed it to Joanna. She tried not to react to it, which was no simple task. She'd never before had a client who handed her a five-figure retainer.

"Umm," she stammered, framing the statement in her mind before finishing the thought. "I don't think I should accept this. If it turns out that either of you is involved in the...involved, then the fact that you paid me could be construed as a conflict of interest."

"My wife and I flew in this morning," Wesley said.

"Tory and I did the same," J.D. said. "Against the advice of her doctor," he added as he glanced over his shoulder at his wife. "Even after a year of marriage my wife hasn't quite grasped the concept of obeying."

"Good for her," Joanna said under her breath, before giving him her best professional smile. "Then I'll deposit this as soon as Mrs. Porter signs this agreement." Joanna slid her retainer agreement to Rose and advised her to read it before signing.

Several minutes passed while Rose, Wesley and then J.D. read the document, then the two men told their mother to sign. Joanna spent the time writing a receipt for the check, which she left on the table. "Whatever charges are incurred by Mr. Langston are—"

"Don't worry about it," Langston cut in.

Joanna turned and met his steely expression. "I don't want there to be any misunderstanding here. I'm not paying you. If the—"

"I said don't worry about it," Langston told her, only this time the words came out like a soft threat. "The check is for your services."

"Ms. Boudreaux does make a good point," J.D. said. "I don't want Shelby or—"

Langston raised one hand. "I said my fee isn't an issue in this case. I think Jo would like it if the two of you gave her some privacy so that she can get to work."

The three men glared at one another for a few seconds before Rose shooed her sons back inside the restaurant. Langston closed the glass doors before joining them at the table.

Today Rose was dressed in a bright-pink blouse, tight green slacks and a belt that had a plastic parrot as the buckle. The parrot motif was repeated in her earrings and the gaudy necklace she was twisting nervously around one finger.

"Gabe, honey, I know Shelby asked you to help out, but I don't want you to get started off here by taking on a charity case."

Langston simply shrugged. "The reason I left the force was so I'd be able to pick and choose my cases. Indulge me here."

"But," Rose argued, "you've only been open a couple of months and I know you've spent a lot of that time in here. I know how it is to start a new business and you'll—"

"Mrs. Porter," Joanna interrupted. "We really do need to get some business done here. Mr. Langston may have nothing better to do than warm your bar stools, but I have less than an hour left.''

Her comment drew sharp looks from both Langston and Rose.

"We need to start with what you said to the police when they arrested you," Joanna went on. "And vice versa."

"Wait a minute," Rose bellowed. "Don't you want to ask me if I did it or not?"

Taking in a breath, Joanna met the woman's wide green eyes. "It isn't my practice to ask clients if they are guilty or not. That information isn't necessary for me to formulate an appropriate defense."

Rose got up so quickly that she toppled her chair. "How the hell can you defend me if you don't know the truth?"

"I know the law, Mrs. Porter. There's a possibility I can get the charges dropped if the police acted improperly either at the time of your arrest or at any time while you were in their custody."

"I didn't kill Joe Don," Rose snapped. "My son just gave you ten thousand dollars to prove that someone else did."

"Actually," Joanna began in a calm, even voice, "this isn't TV or the movies. My job is to first see if I can get the charges dropped, and failing that, to create enough reasonable doubt to keep you from being sent to prison."

"Then I don't want you to represent me," Rose announced as she crossed her arms over her chest.

Joanna sighed and started to reach for the tape recorder's off button. Langston's hand stopped her.

"You want Joanna," he said with a conviction that surprised her. "And—" his eyes fell on Joanna, unblinking "—I'm sure Ms. Boudreaux will work vigorously to prove your innocence."

Slowly Rose righted her chair and sat back down, her expression perplexed. Langston took his hand away from Joanna and placed it on Rose's shoulder. "Just calm down and answer her questions. It's the only way we'll be able to get started on finding the real killer."

Joanna opened her mouth and was about to argue, when Langston sent her a withering look. She should have ignored it. There was no purpose served by letting the woman think she was some sort of real-life female incarnation of Perry Mason. But then, she had ten thousand reasons to follow Langston's lead. The retainer would keep her practice going for quite some time. She could argue the semantics of her responsibilities as defense counsel later.

"The police just showed up at my door at a few minutes after 2 a.m. and told me about Joe Don," Rose began. Her eyes misted over as she continued. "They told me they had a few questions and asked if I would go with them."

"Did they tell you they suspected you in Joe Don's murder then?" Joanna asked.

Rose shook her head. "It wasn't until after I had been there about an hour or so, telling them about Joe

Don and me. Then this detective comes in and starts reading me my rights off some card.''

"Did you ask for an attorney?" Joanna inquired.

Rose scoffed. "Of course not. I hadn't done anything.''

Joanna grabbed the police report from her neatly organized pile and passed it to Rose. "Whatever you tell me is privileged," she said. "That means I can't tell the police or anyone anything you say to me. Do you understand?''

"Of course.''

"Okay." Joanna sighed; then, meeting Langston's eyes, she said, "Technically, you have to be my agent or employee for the privilege to extend to you.''

"Yes, ma'am, boss," he said with a lopsided grin. "Give me a dollar—just to keep this on the up-and-up.''

Joanna pulled her wallet from her purse and flipped the latch to open it. As she did, she heard Langston whisper to Rose.

"Ten bucks says all her money is divided by denomination and all the bills are facing the same way.''

Rose smiled with him.

Defensively, Joanna held her wallet out of the line of their prying eyes and pulled the bill out. She didn't have to look because Langston was right. The ones were neatly arranged in the forward portion of her wallet, just as he had predicted. But she wasn't about to let him know that. "Here," she said as she tossed the dollar in his general direction.

Joanna turned her attention back to Rose. "You told the police that you and Joe Don had dinner together here after closing?"

"Yes."

"And then you went home? Alone?"

Rose's gaze faltered slightly as she said, "Yes, Joe Don said he had a meeting."

"At midnight?"

Rose shrugged. "It had something to do with his new company."

"Where was this meeting supposed to be?" Joanna asked.

"I didn't ask," Rose said.

"Mrs. Porter." Joanna leaned forward. "Rose? I need the truth if I'm going to help you."

Rose's posture was instantly stiff. "I'm telling you the truth."

"Then Susan lied to the police," Joanna explained, flipping to where she had tabbed the waitress's statement. "Because she said she saw you running away when she arrived around one in the morning."

"Susan saw someone," Rose acknowledged, "but it wasn't me."

Joanna took a deep breath. "Rose, you are rather...unmistakable and Susan knows you well."

"But it wasn't me," Rose insisted.

"Why was Susan here in the middle of the night?" Langston asked.

"She had to finish the bank deposit," Rose explained. "She came back to make sure everything was in order for the next morning."

"Does Susan often come back two hours after closing?"

Rose's shoes scuffed against the floor as she answered. "No."

"I've got to tell you," Joanna began as she leaned back in her seat. "It doesn't make sense that on the one night Susan would just happen to be here, your ex-husband is dead in your office. The prosecutor will build his case around all these firsts, and we have to be able to explain them away."

"I can't," Rose admitted. "I only know that I didn't kill Joe Don. We were dating. Trying to see if we had anything in common after all these years apart."

"I'll need you to make a list of anyone and everyone who saw you two together and might be able to testify that you and your ex-husband were on good terms," Joanna explained.

"Okay."

"I'll also need you to write down a full chronology of everything you did in the twenty-four hours prior to the police coming to your door. Include the names and phone numbers of anyone you talked to."

"Okay."

"And don't discuss this with anyone. Not even your sons," Joanna warned. "You talk only to me."

"And me," Langston added.

Joanna gave a grudging nod. "After I have a better

idea of what you did and who you saw, we'll sit down and talk again." She turned to Langston and said, "Would you get Susan now?"

She watched as Langston guided Rose back inside and felt the strain from the interview settle at the top of her spine. Rose hadn't given her much to go on. In her experience, forcing people to write everything down often sparked the memory of some detail that could later prove useful.

The young woman with maroon hair came out with Langston. She looked tired and her shoulders slumped as she took her seat.

Joanna introduced herself and asked, "You told the police that you saw Rose leaving as you came in?"

She nodded. "I called to her, but she didn't turn around. She just jogged up the alley."

"Does Rose usually leave by the alley?" Langston asked.

"She always drives," Susan replied.

"A night of firsts," Joanna grumbled. "Did you see her car at all that night?"

"It was parked right out back while we were open," Susan answered. "It was still parked there when I left after closing."

"What about Mr. Porter?"

Susan shook her head. "I never saw his car. I just assumed he had come with Rose."

"Please don't assume, Susan," Joanna asked with a small smile. "Are you absolutely certain it was Rose in the alley?"

Susan started to cry. "I know it was. I've worked here for almost four years."

"And you have a key?"

The subtle accusation behind the question stopped Susan's tears. "You don't think that I—"

"She has to ask," Langston explained as he patted the slender woman's shoulder.

Reluctantly, Susan lifted her head and met Joanna's eyes, and in a soft, almost apologetic voice, she said, "I knew something terrible was going to happen."

Chapter Three

Gabe watched as Joanna closed her eyes briefly. After Susan's last comment, his attention should have been glued to the waitress, but instead he found himself waiting for Joanna to open her eyes. They reminded him of his favorite diving spot in the Caribbean, at times blue, at others green. Their shape was oddly exotic. Joanna wasn't a classic beauty, not with that flame-red hair and band of faint freckles across the bridge of her small nose. But there was something about the way her features came together on her oval face that held him captivated. And he didn't like it one bit.

Shaking his head, Gabe waited for Susan to further incriminate Rose. "Did you overhear something? Or see something?" he prodded.

The waitress moved her head slowly from side to side. "No, but Joe Don's aura was all off. And my crystals seemed to cool whenever he was in the room."

"Auras and crystals?" Joanna repeated.

Gabe offered her a look that said "Now do you know why the DA doesn't want her underfoot?"

"Rose mentioned you had forgotten to do some paperwork."

"Sort of," Susan hedged.

Hearing the ditsy woman's reluctance, Gabe hoped that she wasn't going to start changing her story. Joanna was right. The DA would be on her like white on rice if she deviated in the slightest from what she had told the police.

Lacing his fingers, Gabe leaned forward, slightly crowding the waitress and garnering her full attention. "You have to tell Joanna what you told the detectives. Try to repeat it exactly."

Susan sniffed before she began to speak. "I came back a little after one."

"Is that when you saw Rose in the alley?" Joanna asked.

Susan nodded. "I let myself in."

"Was the door locked?" Gabe asked.

"Yes, I used my key. I went to the register like she asked and then I started counting out the—"

"Like who asked?" Joanna interrupted.

Susan looked from Joanna to Gabe before softly admitting, "Rose. She called me and told me to come back and do the deposit. She said she'd forgotten and Shelby would be by early to take it to the bank."

"Is that the normal routine?" Joanna queried.

Susan adamantly shook her head. The crystals dangling from the four holes in her ears clinked together with the motion. "She's never called me to do it before that night. If Rose doesn't do it at night, Shelby usually does it when she comes in each morning."

Gabe shared a silent communication with Joanna. He could see her faith in Rose's professed innocence draining away. He couldn't let that happen.

"When did the patrol car arrive?" Gabe asked.

"Maybe five or ten minutes after I got here."

"You didn't call them?" Joanna asked.

He watched as she moistened her finger and flipped through the preliminary report she'd gotten from the authorities.

"But it says here that a woman called in a report of a dead body," Joanna stated.

"Well, it wasn't me," Susan insisted, hugging herself and shivering. "I didn't know he was up there. When I think that I was alone in this place with him up there like that, I get really, *really* stressed."

"Thank you," Joanna said, dismissing her after this bit of information. "I'm sure we'll need to talk again."

"Wait," Gabe said when the waitress began to rise from her chair. "Did you tell anyone you were coming here?"

Susan's brows drew together, as if he'd asked her to explain the theory of relativity. "I wanted Lucy to come with me, but she was asleep."

"Lucy is the one with her nose chained to her ear?" Joanna asked.

"Not really," Susan said, visibly relaxing. "She

does it with magnets. Her nose isn't really pierced. It would limit her professionally if it was."

"Professionally?" Joanna asked.

"She's an actress. She's pretty good, too. She has all of us down to a tee. She does a great Bette Davis."

"That ought to help Rose," Gabe muttered as he forced himself to smile a farewell.

Joanna began placing her things into her briefcase. She kept her eyes averted, but he didn't need to see her face to know what she was thinking. Hell, if he didn't know better, he'd think Rose was guilty, too.

JOANNA'S OFFICE WAS a converted house in the shadows of the Cooper River Bridge. Tammy, her part-time secretary, had left a neat stack of pink messages in the center of her otherwise-clean desk. Joanna sat barefoot in her high-backed leather chair, swaying back and forth as she replayed the interviews in her head. No matter which angle she came from, everything seemed to lead straight back to Rose Porter. She could just hear Harris now, telling the jury that Rose and Joe Don had gone to her office, probably to continue an argument that had started over dinner. Rose killed him in a fit of rage, then called Susan. Hoping the police would find Susan with the body, she then made the anonymous call to the police and raced away. Her one mistake was that Susan, her longtime friend and employee, had seen her fleeing the scene.

"A jury wouldn't be out an hour," she said with a sigh as she twirled herself in a full circle.

"Don't plug in the electric chair just yet."

Startled, Joanna swung back around and was surprised to find Langston framed in her doorway. He had a box of Chinese carryout in one hand and a manila envelope in the other. His expression could only be described as hopeful and energetic. Two things she definitely was not.

"Why are you here?"

Her sharp tone did nothing to deter him. He strode forward and placed the box on her desk, scattering her messages, then pulled one of the chairs closer and sat down with the envelope in his lap.

"I hope you like spicy."

"I don't," she lied. "And I don't recall inviting you here."

Giving her a sidelong glance, he shrugged and tossed her a set of chopsticks. "I work for you. I didn't think I needed an invitation. And I thought you could use some dinner."

"What's in the envelope that has you in such a good mood?" Joanna asked.

He winked. "First we eat, then I'll tell you what's in the envelope."

Brushing some wayward strands of hair off her forehead, Joanna felt her eyes narrow as she glared at him. Her knuckles were almost white from gripping the chopsticks and she was in no mood to play games with him. "I'm not hungry."

His eyes met hers. "Your bottom lip juts out just a little when you lie, Jo."

Having him study her mouth left her feeling vulnerable. A feeling she didn't like.

"Here," he said easily, "try this. It's great."

Joanna hesitated just a second before snatching the carton from him. Somehow she instinctively knew that he wasn't going to reveal the contents of the envelope, no matter how much she argued. He should have been a lawyer, she thought as she took her first mouthful of spicy noodles.

"You have sauce on your chin," he said as he leaned across the desk and rested his palm against the hollow of her cheek. Her lips parted of their own volition as he ran his thumb roughly across her lower lip.

She watched in silence as his eyes fell to her mouth, following each exciting motion of his thumb. The pressure of his hand against her cheek increased as his exploration widened to include her upper lip. Gentle, then building in intensity, his thumb worked a magic against her mouth more ardent and sensual than any kiss. It was so exciting that her breath quickened and her pulse became erratic, carrying the heat of his touch to every cell in her body.

"I think I've taken care of you," he said quietly.

As he pulled his hand away it was everything she could do not to pull it back. She didn't dare speak, certain her words would come out garbled by his near-hypnotic effect on her.

The beep of her organizer broke the spell.

"Reminding you to have dinner?" he teased as he leaned back and contentedly continued to eat.

Joanna was so frazzled that she actually had to pull the thing from her purse and read the display. After doing so, she pressed the button to silence it as she felt her face flame. It was her "get-a-date" reminder.

"Well?"

She didn't meet his eyes when she answered. "Well what?"

"What task have you been commanded to do by that stupid thing?"

Her shoulders stiffened. "It isn't stupid at all. It keeps me from losing focus."

"I'd have thought a bright lady like you would have no troubles staying focused. Fifth in your class, remember?"

"How did you find that out?"

He shrugged his broad shoulders. "I have a friend who has a friend who doesn't mind sharing a little background information from personnel files."

Joanna gaped at him. "You got your information on me from the confidential files in the DA's office?"

His grin was innocent and almost lethal in its charm. "Uh-huh."

"*If* you were a detective, you would know that it is illegal to bribe a public official into giving you information."

There was a definite change in him when she said the word "detective." His whole demeanor seemed to change, and not for the better.

"Well?"

"I was a detective for five of my twelve years on the force."

"Why'd you leave?"

"New York is cold."

"Maybe, but the pay had to be better than what you can make working as a PI."

"Money isn't the most important thing in the world."

Joanna let her head fall to one side as she studied him. "Then I was right about you."

"Right about what?"

"The only people who wax philosophic about money are the people who have more of it than they need."

"Money doesn't make you happy, Jo."

"But the lack of it can certainly make life hell," she countered. "So, are you just well-off or filthy rich?"

His dark head went back and he laughed aloud. "I don't think any woman has ever been quite so up-front about the issue before."

She smiled in spite of herself. "Is that your way of trying to get me to believe that women are only interested in you for your money?"

"Can you think of another reason?" he teased, though there was an underlying seriousness to his tone.

"Not really," she answered. Of course, it didn't take a rocket scientist to know she was lying, but

Langston seemed willing to let it pass. "So, when do I get to find out what's in your secret envelope?"

"Patience isn't one of your virtues, is it, Jo?"

She bristled at his incessant use of that nickname. "Look, Langston, I'm tired and I do have things to do."

"Your purse isn't beeping."

"Cute," she grumbled.

"I'll make you a deal," he offered with a wicked twinkle in his eyes.

"What kind of deal?"

"Are you always this cautious?"

"Are you always this difficult?"

"Okay," he said with a shrug. "I'll let you have the envelope if you say my name."

Joanna sighed. "Langston, I've not only said your name, I've cursed it several times."

"My first name."

"Gabriel."

He glared at her. "I told you that my friends call me 'Gabe.'"

She glared back. "I know. So, now do I get to see the envelope?"

"You didn't do what I asked."

"I said your first name. I don't recall there being any codicils as to form or content."

"God, you do sound like a lawyer."

"And you sound like a spoiled child. Either give me the envelope, or take your Chinese smorgasbord and leave me alone so I can do some work."

He tossed the envelope onto her desk with just the right amount of force for it to come sliding to a halt just shy of falling into her lap.

"How did you get this stuff?" Joanna asked as she scanned the documents.

"I have lots of friends."

She lifted her eyes to his. "Now that you're my employee, if you break the law, I'll be held accountable. Harris will have a fit if he knows—"

"Harris knows," he cut in. "The forensics report is a public document. I simply went down and had copies made at the same time they were running off a set for the DA's office. Harris has to give you all that as part of discovery. I just saved him the headache."

"I doubt he'll feel that way," Joanna said on a breath. She could just imagine her former boss raging when he got word that she was getting information just as easily as he was. "I don't know why you think this is helpful," she said as she flipped through the first few pages.

"Skip everything else and get to the last page."

Joanna did as he instructed at the same time the fax machine in the outer office buzzed and started spewing paper. "Putty?" she said as she read from the crime tech's report. "They found putty on his clothing and on the desk?"

"Along with gunpowder residue," he finished.

"But they did a test on Rose and she was negative for residue, same as Susan."

"Which goes a long way to support Rose's claim that she didn't shoot her ex."

"You have selective retention, Langston. The report also says that Rose is the registered owner of a .22, which is the same caliber of gun used in the killing and is now conveniently missing. It also says that they haven't finished running tests on clothing taken from Rose's home when they executed a search warrant today."

"Are you always so quick to jump on the negative? Rose needs you in her corner."

"What Rose needs," Joanna said through tight lips, "is for everyone around her to be a little more honest."

"Meaning?" he asked in a tone as argumentative as Joanna's.

"C'mon, Langston. If you know anything about law enforcement, then surely you know that the police are right about ninety-eight percent of the time. Rose had the means, the motive and the opportunity to commit the murder, and there was an eyewitness. Hell, a first-year law school student could get a conviction."

She watched as his features seemed to darken into a very pronounced scowl. "If you don't believe she's innocent, why did you take the case?"

"My job isn't to judge her guilt or innocence," Joanna shot back. "My job is to make sure she's treated fairly by the system."

"Your job is to get her off because she isn't guilty."

"How can you be so sure?" she asked. "You've only known her a couple of months. I appreciate the fact that you like the food at the Rose Tattoo, but I can hardly stand up in court and say, 'Ladies and gentlemen of the jury, Rose Porter makes a mean martini and excellent light red sauce, so please return a verdict of not guilty.'"

Joanna thought for a brief second that they could come to blows over the subject. Langston was so tightly coiled that she could make out the definition in his well-muscled upper body.

"So, you're just the keeper of the Constitution, is that it? Are you that lacking in principle?"

Joanna jumped up and tossed the pages at him, too furious to speak. Needing to get away from him before she hit him with her shoe or something equally stupid, she breezed past him into the outer office. She grabbed the fax pages out of the tray, stopping to sort them on Tammy's desk. The few bites she had taken of the food fell like a rock in the pit of her stomach as she read.

"Hey, Langston!" she called out.

He was at her side in an instant, towering over her now that she didn't have the advantage of her heels.

"What?"

"Here," she said, slamming the pages against his solid chest. "It's a supplement from Harris's office. Maybe you'd better go ask the innocent ex-Mrs. Porter why they found the deceased Mr. Porter's car on the street a block from her apartment."

"I'm sure she'll have a reasonable explanation."

"Good," Joanna said with an exaggerated nod. "Because they found her gun inside it, complete with her fingerprints."—

Chapter Four

The scent of wisteria blossoms surrounded Joanna as she stood next to her car in the harsh early-morning sun. It was going to be one of those hot, miserably oppressive days. She could feel perspiration trickling between her shoulder blades as she shed her pale-yellow jacket.

Cursing under her breath, she leaned against her car and allowed her purse to fall to the ground next to her feet. "Where the hell are you?" she grumbled.

Joanna shoved her sunglasses against her face as she stared at the locked gate of the impound lot. A sign wired to the fence read Open 7:00 a.m. to 4:30 p.m. Only it was fifteen before eight, and Joanna's annoyance intensified with each passing second.

Pulling her cell phone from her briefcase, Joanna pressed a series of buttons from memory. The telephone rang three times before a breathy female voice said, "Hello."

"Trisha?" Joanna asked.

"Yep, I'm running late," Trisha confessed. "Are you okay?"

"Basically," Joanna told her longtime friend. "I need a favor."

"I hope it's a quick one."

"It is," Joanna promised. "I need information on a Gabriel Langston."

"What sort of information?" Trisha asked cautiously. "Is he a client?"

"No. He's kind of like an employee."

Trisha's laughter filled her ears.

"Right."

"What is that supposed to mean?"

"You really should read the society pages, Joanna," Trisha admonished. "Gabriel Langston was the only son and heir to Langston Publishing. He sold the company to some international conglomerate about six months ago."

"How do you know all that?" Joanna asked.

"'Cause my firm spent more than a year trying to woo him away from Halsted-McGregor."

"Any luck?"

"Nope. The man's rumored to be very loyal. And incredibly gorgeous."

"That part is true," Joanna admitted. "Was he really a cop up there?"

"Yep," Trisha answered. "Apparently he went against his father's wishes and joined the force. For years there were rumors that the old man was going to disinherit him because Gabriel showed no interest in the publishing empire.''

''And?''

''And that turned out to be just a rumor. Of course, when he sold the company even nastier rumors started.''

''Why?''

''C'mon, Joanna. You're making me late for a meeting.''

''Sorry,'' she murmured.

There was a brief silence before Trisha sighed and said, ''Gabriel Langston made a fortune selling off the family business, and it didn't sit too well with the relatives.''

''They wanted to keep the company in the family?''

''That and supposedly the uncles and cousins resented Gabriel from the get-go.''

''The man does have a talent for grating on your nerves.''

''It wasn't about his personality. It was about his parentage.''

''Meaning?''

''Gabriel was adopted by the old man and his wife. The family never accepted him.''

After saying a quick goodbye, Joanna was totally lost in thought when a pencil-necked guy whom she placed in his late teens sauntered up to the padlock and finally opened the gate. While Trisha's revelations confirmed a lot of what Joanna already knew, it also gave her a new perspective on the man. Much as she didn't want to, she felt herself softening her opinion just a tad. Thanks to loving parents, Joanna had experienced the picture-perfect childhood. Envisioning Langston as a small child, shunned and helpless against a resentful crop of relatives, tugged at her heartstrings.

"You coming in or what?" the guy called to her.

Retrieving her purse, Joanna pulled out her business card as well as a copy of the fax Harris had sent to her the previous night.

The young man barely glanced at her papers before shrugging and going into a small building. She heard a radio come on a second or so after he opened the door. She watched his back as he looked from her paper to a pegboard filled with ticket stubs and keys.

"Aren't we up bright and early?"

Joanna turned toward the voice, tilting her head back as she peered up at him from behind the safety of her sunglasses. Langston was positively gorgeous in his butter-soft jeans and crisp, white polo shirt. Seemingly expensive loafers completed the outfit, but he looked anything but casual. There was something about the way he moved that gave him an air of preparedness, like a predatory cat waiting to move in for the kill.

He pulled his sunglasses down, allowing them to rest near the end of his nose, and peered at her over the rounded rims. "You aren't speaking today, Jo?"

"It's early, Langston," she countered. Her chilled

tone managed to erase the smug half smile from his lips. "I didn't think people like you did mornings."

"Like me?" It was his turn to speak in a frosty tone.

Joanna shrugged. "The idle rich."

"I've never been idle," he said tightly.

"But you are rich."

His eyes narrowed slightly and Joanna was glad she had sunglasses to hide behind. She almost flinched at the hostility she saw in his hardened expression.

"And where did you get your information?"

"I didn't get information. I simply have a friend who lives in Manhattan, and she seemed to know a great deal about you."

He glared for a few more seconds before he asked, "How much did she tell you?"

"Enough for me to know that you are some sort of crusader and Rose Porter, for whatever reason, is your latest cause."

His mouth curved into a rather annoying and definitely superior smile. "If your friend told you I was some sort of crusader, I'm afraid she doesn't know what she's talking about."

"What do you call a man who risks a fortune to be a cop?"

"A man who chooses his own life."

Bested again, she thought as the smaller man emerged from the shed with a ticket in one hand and her papers in the other.

"Fourth row," he said as he handed Joanna the papers and Langston the ticket. "Seventh car down."

She struggled to keep up with him, silently cursing her pointed-toed pumps as she kept her eyes fixed on his broad shoulders. Walking behind him, Joanna had no choice but to inhale the masculine scent of his cologne. She tried holding her breath, deep breathing, anything that might counter the distracting effect his scent seemed to have on her pulse. It wasn't the same mind-numbing rush of sensation she'd experienced when he'd touched her last night. However, she did concede that just being near him had a real and immediate effect on her system. He was exactly the kind of man she despised. Far too arrogant and far too handsome.

"This is it," he said as they came up to an older import.

He opened the driver's side door and Joanna slipped inside. "How tall is Rose?"

"About five-five," he answered. "Why?"

Shoving her glasses up on her head, she threw down her purse and reached for the wheel. Her hands fell far short. "Does she have arms like an orangutan?"

"Not that I've noticed," he answered. "You know," he began as he bunched the legs of his jeans and squatted next to her. "They could have moved the seat when they did the forensics."

Joanna felt her spirits plummet.

"Careful, Jo," he said smoothly as his hand came to rest on top of her knee.

She almost jumped at the contact. It took all her composure not to react to the way his fingers curled around her knee, burning the sensitive flesh near the joint.

"For a minute there, you sounded like you believed in Rose."

"It was an observation, Langston," she said, fixing her eyes on the pollen and fingerprint dust covering the sun-faded vinyl interior. "Anything I can use to sprinkle doubt on Harris's case is worth noting."

Joanna reached out, and using her forefinger and thumb, she lifted his hand by the wrist and tossed it aside. "I would think that a veteran of law enforcement would know better than to assume a criminal defendant was innocent."

The hand she had tossed away was on her again, only this time he gripped her upper arm, pinching the flesh beneath the fabric of her blouse.

"How did you get so cynical in such a short time?"

"Not cynical, realistic," she answered as she gave her arm a futile tug. She kept her eyes fixed straight ahead. "I would think you'd be just a tad less Pollyannalike yourself after a dozen years on the force."

"I'm hardly that," he said. "And since I've known Rose longer than you have, I would think you would defer to my judgment when it comes to this."

Joanna looked at him then. Actually, she whipped

her head around and stared at her reflection in his glasses. "Do you have anything besides your biased opinion of the woman?" she challenged. "Or do you think I can go into court and say, 'Forget all the evidence. Langston thinks she's innocent'?"

"No, I expect you to develop your own evidence that will lead us to the real killer."

"Thank you, Paul Drake," she grumbled as she shoved him back. The push forced him to release her arm in order to brake his fall as he landed squarely on his rear end. Joanna got out of the car, tossed her purse onto her shoulder and began stiffly walking back through the lot.

"You owe me an apology."

"Go away, Langston," she replied without looking at him. "I don't think you're going to be much help to me. I need someone who isn't seeing this through rose-colored glasses—no pun intended."

GABE STRADDLED the stool of the bar at the Rose Tattoo before lowering himself down next to Wesley Porter. Lucy was behind the bar, dressed in gaudy sixties retro clothing. She smiled as she came up to him, winking playfully with eyes drenched in a light-blue powder; her lips were frosted white.

"Hi, Gabe, what can I get you?"

Glancing at his watch, he grinned at the habit. His father had been quite a stickler about not drinking before five. It was ten after, so he ordered a scotch, neat.

In the mirror behind the rows of liquor bottles, he watched the door. It wasn't like her to be late.

"Waiting for someone?" Wesley asked just as Lucy placed his drink on a napkin in front of him.

"Joanna was supposed to meet me here at five."

He watched as the man's expression grew unreadable. "Why is she coming back?"

"She's Rose's attorney," Gabe answered as he took a sip of his drink and let it burn a path to his stomach.

"Not if I can help it," Wesley muttered.

"What are you talking about?" Gabe asked as he met the other man's eyes.

"J.D. is upstairs with Mom and that Boudreaux woman right now. Hopefully J.D. will convince Mother to—"

"That was a stupid move," Gabe said as he grabbed his drink and stormed past Susan.

Taking the back stairs two at a time, Gabe reached the second floor in no time. He followed the angry voices down the hall, until he reached the office door.

"Is far more qualified."

Rose glared at J.D., her green eyes narrowed and angry. "I don't give a flaming fig how qualified the man is I don't want to pay some fool thousands of dollars to—"

"I'll be paying," J.D. interrupted.

"Like hell," Rose shot right back.

"If your son has no faith in me," Joanna began in

a tight voice, "then perhaps it would be best if I stepped aside."

Gabe watched from the hallway as she drew herself up with admirable dignity. She took only one step, when Rose reached out and grasped the sleeve of her jacket. J.D.'s back was to him, but Gabe could tell by his wide stance and clenched hands that the man was battling for control.

"Wait a minute," Rose said. "I hired you and I'm not going to fire you and Gabe."

"That's another problem," J.D. yelled. "The man has no connections here in Charleston. For God's sake, Mother. The bozo has only lived here a couple of months."

It was at that instant that his eyes found Joanna's. She looked positively stricken, so much so that Rose and J.D. followed her line of sight, and saw him in the shadow of the doorway.

"Gabe," Rose began as she shot her son a withering look. "Don't mind J.D. I'm sure he learned his rudeness from that coed his father married after me."

Gabe shrugged and winked at Rose. The look he offered J.D. was much less charitable. He took a couple of steps forward as he reached into the breast pocket of his jacket.

Meeting the other man's baleful look, he tossed several pictures onto the desk near where Joanna stood. "Bozo brought gifts for the crowd."

"Apologize, J.D.," Rose prompted.

"No need," Gabe assured her. He turned to Joanna

and said, "I followed up on your hunch about the car."

"What hunch?" J.D. asked.

"They didn't move the seat?" Joanna asked.

"What seat?" J.D. asked.

"I spoke to the crime-scene tech myself," Gabe continued, pointedly ignoring the man as he moved next to Joanna under the guise of examining the pictures with her. "They searched the car, did it for prints, but he swears the seat was all the way back when they brought him the car."

"What about the officers who found it?" Joanna asked him.

God, when she looked up at him like that it did strange things to his blood pressure. He tried not to think about the way her hair caught the last few rays of the setting sun. He tried, but he wasn't very successful. Now as he watched, transfixed, she drew her bottom lip between her teeth. She bit down, then slowly allowed her lip to slide back into place. It glistened with moisture.

He swallowed a groan.

"Well?" she prompted.

"Do the two of you mind telling me what you're going on about?" Rose demanded.

Reluctantly, he tore his eyes away from Joanna's supple mouth and gazed at Rose. "We went to the impound yard and Joanna noticed that your car seat was all the way back. Unless your legs have extenders, I think Joanna is onto something."

He had expected Rose to look relieved, maybe even excited. Instead she lowered her eyes and moved away, behind her desk.

"What is it?" Gabe asked.

Joanna stepped forward, placed her fingertips on the desk and said, "You were lying, weren't you?"

"I was..."

"Dammit, Rose!" Joanna yelled, slamming her fists down on the desk. "I can't defend you if you don't tell me the truth."

"I haven't lied to you," Rose said.

"I asked you yesterday when you last saw Joe Don," Joanna said.

"You don't need to yell at her," J.D. said.

Before Gabe could utter a word in her defense, Joanna spun on the balls of her feet, squared her small frame and looked up at Rose's son with pure fury in her aqua eyes. Gabe crossed his arms in front of his chest, fully prepared to enjoy Joanna chewing out that arrogant jackass.

"You are here on suffrage," Joanna thundered.

"I wrote the check."

"So stop payment," Joanna shot back at him. "Or better still, if it means I don't have to put up with your disparaging my abilities or the abilities of Mr. Langston, I'll refund your money. I'm not so desperate for work that I have to stand here and have my skills trashed by you."

"I didn't mean—"

"Spare me," Joanna interrupted. "What *did* you

mean when you said that you had spoken to another firm about taking your mother's case? It sure as hell didn't sound like an endorsement of your faith in me, Mr. Porter. So, since I sat here quietly while you tried to convince your mother that I wasn't qualified to defend her, you can listen to my assessment of you. You seem to be under the impression that I need or require your approval in order to defend your mother. I can assure you, I do not. I also do not have any intention of begging to stay on this case, so—"

Joanna grabbed her bag and briefcase and he noted her hands were completely steady.

"—I'll have my secretary write out a refund less the hours I have already spent on this matter. Have whomever you hire contact me and I'll turn over all my notes."

Joanna brushed past him without hesitation. He was left standing in the room with a very surprised J.D. and a very angry Rose.

Gabe walked over to Shelby's desk, downed the last of his scotch and hoisted himself onto the desk. "That was well-handled, J.D. I doubt any of the senior partners at those huge firms will argue Rose's case with the fire and passion Joanna has."

"Stay out of this," the other man yelled.

"J.D.!" Rose cried. "The only thing I want you to do is shag your butt downstairs and catch her before she makes good on her threat and quits."

"Mother!"

"Move," Rose told her son in a tone that all but dared him to argue.

"You're making a mistake," J.D. grumbled as he left the room.

"Not like the one you just made," Gabe said to the man's back.

"Don't bait him," Rose chided. "He's just looking out for me."

"His attitude might just cost you Joanna's representation," Gabe told her.

"*His* attitude," Rose said with a mirthless little laugh. "You aren't much better at times."

"This isn't about me," Gabe said. "This is about you."

"I figured that out when they fingerprinted me."

Gabe cocked his head and regarded the woman. "Joanna is a fighter, Rose. She's effective in the courtroom."

"How do you know?"

"I did some checking when Shelby gave me her name. The woman has only lost three of her last fifteen cases."

"That's something," Rose mumbled as she fell into her chair.

Gabe noticed how tired she looked. "Are you sleeping?"

"Not well."

"You should see your doctor, tell him what's happening."

"My doctor is a her," Rose said. "And the last

thing I need is to fog up my brain with sleeping pills.''

''But if you can't sleep...'' He allowed the thought to hang in the air between them.

''I'll sleep just fine once all this is behind me.''

''WELL.'' Joanna's voice arrived just a split second before she did. ''All this won't be behind you until you start telling the truth.''

Leaning against the doorjamb, Joanna looked at Langston briefly before turning her attention completely on her client. Rose wouldn't meet her stare—not a good sign.

''We can start with the gun,'' Joanna suggested.

''I don't know how it got into the car.''

''Where was it usually kept?''

''Downstairs near the register,'' Rose said.

''Out in plain sight?'' Gabe asked.

''Of course not,'' Rose huffed. She patted the side of her overteased hair as she spoke.

The action reminded Joanna of Lucy. Today the bartender resembled some reject from Rowan and Martin's ''Laugh-In.'' She had caught only brief glimpses of Lucy, but that was all she needed. Between Lucy and her Look-of-the-Day and Susan's auras and crystals, Joanna wondered how the apparently normal Rose and Shelby could stand working with such a strange staff.

''It was in a lockbox,'' Rose explained.

''Which is?'' Gabe asked.

"Downstairs, right where it should be, only the gun isn't inside."

"That's convenient," Joanna breathed. "When was the last time you saw it?"

Rose looked to the ceiling, then back at Joanna. "Are you sure you want to know?"

"I'm sure."

"It was in the lockbox on the day Joe Don was murdered."

Chapter Five

"Do you believe her?" Gabe asked as he walked with her toward the front door.

"It sounds a little far-fetched."

"Shelby backed her up," Gabe reminded her.

"Shelby isn't an unbiased witness," Joanna reminded him. "And she left the Rose Tattoo long before Rose did, which makes her statement that the gun was locked behind the bar at 4 p.m. completely irrelevant."

"You really are the soothsayer of doom."

Joanna ignored the barb. Gabe blocked her path and stood before her with his hand out, palm up. "What?"

"Your keys?"

"I can see myself in, Langston."

"I'm sure you can," he replied without moving his hand or his massive body.

"You and J. D. Porter are cut from the same cloth," she grumbled as she dropped her key chain into his palm. "Remember, you insisted."

"Thank you. And Porter and I are nothing alike," he retorted as he unlocked the door.

She hung back on the first step, silently counting. She reached sixty just as the alarm began blaring.

"What's the code?" he yelled over the deafening sound.

Shaking her head and unable to keep the smile from her face, Joanna stepped inside and pressed the keypad to stop the alarm. Almost instantly, the telephone rang. Dropping her briefcase and purse on Tammy's desk, she grabbed the receiver and told the alarm company her password and said everything was fine.

"That wasn't nice," he admonished as he sat in one of the chairs in the reception area.

"It wasn't supposed to be," she retorted with a little laugh. "But that's what happens when you act before thinking. I mean, there are stickers in the windows, Langston."

"Are you always so disagreeable?"

Joanna gave him a saccharine smile. "You do seem to bring out the worst in me."

He rose slowly, moving silently to suddenly crowd her space. He loomed above her, motionless. He didn't have to move; she could feel his heat, smell the scent that seemed to awaken something deep in the pit of her stomach.

She was saved when the telephone rang.

"Hello."

"Ms. Boudreaux, this is Shelby Tanner."

"Hi, Shelby, what can I do for you?"

"I think you'd better turn the television on."

"Why?" Joanna asked, hearing the sound of a small child crying in the background.

"I've got to see to Cassidy," Shelby answered. "Just turn on the news."

"What is it?" Langston asked, even before Joanna had placed the receiver on the cradle.

"Something on the news," she told him, then headed for the stairs, aware of the fact that he was following her.

The second floor of the building was her home. She went into her bedroom, grabbed the remote control and turned the set on.

She fell onto the end of her neatly made bed as she clicked through a series of channels before finding the special bulletin. "Great," she groaned as she felt Langston sit next to her. His weight caused her shoulder to brush against his arm.

"...husband was a good and caring man," the woman said as she dabbed tears from her doelike eyes.

Beneath the sympathy-arousing image of the tall blonde the station had typed out her name—Shelia Porter, wife of murder victim Joseph Don Porter.

"I've come to see that my husband's killer is punished," she announced. "I've already spoken with District Attorney Harris and he has assured me that his office has an airtight case against that horrid creature."

The newspeople had timed it just right. Shelia had just uttered the words "horrid creature," when a tape of Rose being led, shackled, into the police station flashed on the screen.

"So much for a fair trial," Joanna grumbled.

"Will you move for a change of venue?" Langston asked.

"I won't get it," Joanna said without looking at him. "Harris will simply tell the judge that we can get a fair trial by weeding out potential problem jurors in voir dire."

"She's threatened to kill him on more than one occasion in the past," Shelia continued. "I warned him not to come to Charleston. Not with that crazy ex-wife of his."

"Mrs. Porter, will you be attending the hearing in the morning?" a reporter asked.

"Of course. There's no telling who she'll go after next. She's threatened me, as well. She never accepted the fact that Joseph left her and won custody of their sons."

"What about her sons?" was the follow-up question.

"We're very close. I practically raised them, since Rose had no interest in her children."

"Turn it off," Langston grumbled.

"I'll bet Harris arranged this," Joanna said as she punched the button to turn off the television.

"What do you know about Shelia?" he asked.

Joanna sighed. "Obviously not enough. But that

can be easily rectified." She tossed the remote onto the middle of the bed and reached for the telephone. In just over ten minutes, she knew the name of Shelia's hotel, courtesy of the reserved Wesley Porter.

"I'd love to know why I'm so unpopular with Rose's sons," Joanna said as she and Langston returned to the first floor.

"Don't let it bother you," he said.

As his large hand reached the center of her back, she could feel the heat of his touch through her clothing, and mentally hated herself for being so aware of the man. How could such an innocent gesture wreak such havoc with her senses? This acute awareness was like nothing she had ever experienced before. But why? It wasn't as though she led some cloistered life and she was desperate.

"What are we going to do?" he asked.

"You're going home, or whatever it is you do," she responded as she collected her briefcase and her purse. "I'm going to pay a visit to Shelia."

"Do you think that's smart?" he asked as he placed his hand on her shoulder.

Joanna looked up into his hazel eyes. "Rose has a bail review hearing in the morning. I have no intention of being blindsided by the grieving wife."

"I'll come with you."

"That isn't necessary," she argued. "Wesley said he would call her and convince her to see me."

"I'm coming."

Joanna let out an exasperated sigh. "Why?"

"Because for all you know, Shelia could be the killer. It's my job to protect you."

Frowning, she asked, "Since when?"

"Since yesterday. Since you let me touch you."

Joanna lowered her eyes and felt her face grow warm and her heart skip several beats. "I let you wipe food off my lip. That puts you in the same category as a napkin."

His hand moved from her shoulder, down to the center of her back. In a flash, Joanna found herself plastered against him with her arms trapped at her sides.

"Joanna," he said in a quiet command. "Look at me."

"Let go of me."

"No."

Stiffening, she slowly tilted her head back until she felt the warmth of his breath washing across her up-turned face. "I've looked, so let me go."

He smiled. "Why do you get so strange whenever I touch you?"

"Maybe it's because you touch me without my permission."

He chuckled. The action caused his massive chest to move against her, making her far too conscious of his maleness.

"I'm sorry if it bothers you," he said with absolutely no remorse to reinforce the statement. "I can't help it if I like to touch you."

"That's ridiculous," she scoffed. "You're an

adult. Surely you're capable of a small amount of self-control.''

His hand ran up her arm until his palm rested against the side of her throat. Joanna was sure he could feel the erratic beat of her pulse.

''What if I don't want to control myself?'' he asked in a soft, sensual tone that made her legs feel like jelly.

''Then learn,'' she stated forcefully as she stepped out of his embrace. ''Try to remember that your job is to investigate a murder. Not to smooth-talk your way into bed with me.''

She had expected him to lash out at her. Instead he simply smiled. Well, the smile wasn't exactly a simple action. No, it was the smile of a man gladly and arrogantly accepting a challenge.

Joanna turned and went to Tammy's desk, flipping on the computer and trying not to notice that Langston had come up behind her as she typed appropriate information into the form document.

''Smart move,'' he commented as the laser printer spewed out a crisp sheet of paper.

''If Shelia is reluctant to talk to me, maybe this will make her a little more cooperative.''

''NICE DIGS,'' Gabe said as he held the door open for Joanna.

The Omni hotel in downtown Charleston was a prestigious address. He had been a resident there when he'd first arrived in the city. The nightly charges were in keeping with the five-star rating, which told him that Shelia wasn't hard up for cash.

When the elevator doors closed, Gabe turned to Joanna's profile. God, she was beautiful, he thought as his eyes roamed over every inch of her face. He had to stop thinking along these lines. Especially if he was going to be of any help to Rose. Maybe he should get himself one of those annoying organizers. He could set it at fifteen-minute intervals to remind him that his focus was Rose, not the stunning redhead with the nervous habit of biting her lower lip.

"If Shelia can afford this, how come Joe Don was living in a rented room in North Charleston?" he asked as the elevator stopped on the penthouse floor.

Joanna stopped and met his eyes. "You're loaded and yet you have an office next door to an orphanage."

"I like the location," he said as he averted his eyes. "My office is central to everything."

"To bars, restaurants and the straw market."

"You're pretty critical of my office for someone who has never seen it," he said as he guided her toward the end of the poshly carpeted hallway.

"I saw it from the window of the Rose Tattoo," she countered as she reached one dainty hand out to knock on the door. "I would have thought you'd have gone for one of those new office parks off the Mark Clark."

He winked down at her. "Then I guess you'll have

to get to know me better so you'll stop jumping to these wrong conclusions.''

She had opened her mouth, no doubt ready to toss a criticism at him, when the door opened and they were met by a hostile pair of clear blue eyes.

His first impression of Shelia was that she reminded him of one of his aunts. The statuesque blonde was wearing a flowing robe in a pale pink, and matching backless heeled slippers. Her face was enhanced by a healthy amount of expertly applied makeup. She looked more like an aging model than a grieving widow. But he knew her type. She had her nails done religiously and probably had shoes to match every outfit. Appearance was everything.

''I'm talking to you only as a favor to my stepsons,'' Shelia announced curtly as she showed them into the sitting area of her suite. ''Mr. Harris said you would probably harass me.''

''I'm just here to interview you, Mrs. Porter,'' Joanna said as she pulled her recorder and a legal pad from her briefcase. ''It shouldn't take too much of your time.''

''I have funeral arrangements to see to,'' Shelia said as a handkerchief appeared in her hand and she dabbed at her eyes. ''This is a very difficult time for me.''

''I'm sure it is,'' Joanna said, without a great deal of sympathy in her tone. ''You and Mr. Porter were married for how long?''

''Nearly twenty-eight years,'' she answered. ''Joseph was my instructor in college. I was quite young when we married.''

"And you raised J.D. and Wesley?'' Gabe asked.

Shelia looked at him then, as if she just noticed he was in the room. Her visual appraisal took a few seconds, and encompassed every inch of Gabe's frame—hardly an action appropriate to her role as grieving widow.

"The boys came to live with us when they were small. Rose was a horrid mother and—''

"Rose isn't charged with being a bad parent,'' Joanna cut in. "You said in your interview with the press that you and Mr. Porter received death threats from Mrs. Porter?''

Gabe watched Shelia's expression grow immediately hostile.

"*I'm* Mrs. Porter,'' she said with undisguised venom dripping from each carefully uttered syllable.

"Of course,'' Joanna said, unfazed. "Could you give me some information on these threats?''

"They started when Joseph and I began living together.''

Joanna turned her head and communicated her surprise. Gabe leaned forward, resting his elbows on his knees as he eyed the woman seated across from them. She sat stiffly in the chair, gripping the armrests so hard that her knuckles were beginning to turn white. She looked every bit like a queen upon her throne.

"That was a long time ago,'' Gabe stated. "Has Rose made any threats more recently?''

"She was pressuring Joseph."

"Pressuring how?" he asked.

"When she found out that Joseph and I were communicating regularly, she had a problem with that."

"How was your relationship with Mr. Porter?" Joanna asked.

Shelia's confident facade wavered slightly as she squirmed in her throne. Gabe's police instincts kicked in as he listened to what her body language was saying.

"Joseph and I had a few problems. What couple doesn't? Especially when you've been married as long as we were."

"Why did Mr. Porter come to Charleston?" Joanna pressed.

"He wanted to expand his business up here. He was an architect and a builder. He was tired of doing planned communities in Miami, so he decided to come up here to work on remodeling and rehabbing older homes. He simply wanted some new challenges."

"So he comes to the city where his ex-wife lives?" Gabe asked.

Shelia was struggling to keep her anger in check. He knew that much from the way her fists tightened on the chair.

"He came here because Charleston was his home. He had as much right to be here as she did."

"And that was when?" Joanna asked. "When exactly did Mr. Porter move to Charleston?"

Shelia got to her feet. "He didn't move here," she sputtered. "This was all temporary."

"Is that why you didn't accompany him?" Joanna pressed.

Shelia paced behind her chair. "We have a home and obligations in Florida, Ms. Boudreaux. I stayed behind to see to those things."

"When was the last time you spoke to Joe Don?" Gabe asked.

"His name was 'Joseph,'" Shelia informed him tautly before she blinked enough to fill her eyes with moisture. "We talked the afternoon before he was killed."

"Did he say anything about a business meeting?" Joanna asked.

Shelia stilled and said, "Not to me. If he had a business meeting, he would have told me about it. Joseph and I didn't have any secrets."

"Then you knew he was seeing Rose on a regular basis?" Joanna asked with just the right amount of "suck-on-that" in her tone.

"I don't know where you got an idea like that. Joseph was going to return to Florida. He told me so when I spoke to him."

"So, your separation wasn't permanent?" Gabe asked.

"It wasn't a separation," Shelia insisted. "Joseph and I were happily married."

"Oh," Joanna remarked innocently as she reached for her briefcase.

Gabe had to hide his admiration, guessing what she was about to do.

Joanna tossed a photograph on the glass coffee table that separated them from the now-nervous woman. "Can you explain that?"

"Get out!" Shelia barked as she turned her back on the unpleasant photograph of Joe Don's body slumped at Rose's desk. "I can't believe you'd be so calloused as to show me that."

"I do apologize," Joanna said, "but there wasn't time before tomorrow's hearing for me to isolate the part of the photo I'd like for you to explain."

Shelia turned around and glared at Joanna. "How can I possibly explain anything that went on that night, when I wasn't even there?"

Joanna placed her legal pad so that it covered the part of the picture that showed Joe Don's injuries. "Take a look, Mrs. Porter," Joanna persisted. "Here," she added, pointing to a part of the photograph.

Shelia wasn't exactly cooperative, Gabe decided. Leaning over the back of the chair, she gave just a cursory look to where Joanna held her finger.

"There's some sort of box in his hand," she said. "So what? What could that possibly have to do with me?"

"You said that you and Mr. Porter were happily married."

"Yes," Shelia hissed.

"Then I guess this was a gift for you?"

"What gift?" Shelia asked as she came around and took a closer look at the present. "I have no idea what you're talking about."

"Well—" Joanna sighed as she took Gabe's arm and forced him to his feet along with her "—I'm sorry to have intruded on your...grief."

Joanna had collected her pad and was reaching for the picture, when Shelia grabbed it and stared for several minutes. "I suppose Joseph could have been planning to mail this down to me."

"With that pretty bow on it?" Joanna asked. "And then there's the card with it."

"What card?" Shelia asked, her face suddenly filled with panic. "What card?" she demanded more forcefully.

"There was a card recovered with the gift," Joanna explained. "I guess I forgot the picture that shows the card. I'm sorry we bothered you," Joanna said again as she held out her hand for the return of the photo. "We'll be on our way."

"Not until you tell me about the card," Shelia fairly shrieked.

Joanna's smile was deceptively pleasant as she regarded the taller woman. "I'm sure you're right, Mrs. Porter. I'm sure the gift was for you."

"What was it?" Shelia demanded.

"A small gold chain," Joanna answered. "Herringbone, I think. Ten-karat electroplate."

Gabe followed Joanna's gaze to the diamond-and-gold necklace around Shelia's neck. Shelia countered by placing her hand at her throat.

"A bit of a comedown from what you're obviously used to," Joanna remarked blandly. "Now, if you'd be kind enough to return the photograph, we'll be on our way."

"Tell me what the card said," Shelia insisted as she gripped the picture in her hand.

"I don't remember offhand," Joanna said. "Do you recall what it said?"

Gabe, following her lead, shrugged and stroked his chin. He could almost feel Shelia's anxiety as he stalled.

"Oh, yes," Joanna said as she tapped her forehead. "It was blank on the outside."

Shelia seemed to visibly relax.

"The inside was pretty sentimental, I think."

"What?" Shelia wailed. "What did it say?"

"I'm sure the police will turn it over to you once it's no longer needed for evidence."

When Joanna turned away from Shelia, she gave him just the smallest nod before she reached into her briefcase.

"I remember now," Gabe said. "Joe Don had written 'For everything you've done for me' on the inside."

Joanna pulled her hand out of the briefcase, extracting the hastily typed document in the process. She folded it neatly before saying, "Since you and

Mr. Porter were so happily married, I'm sure the gift was meant for you.''

Shelia was just standing there, her expression blank. Joanna seized the opportunity and snatched the photograph out of her hand and put the subpoena in its place.

''What the hell is this?'' Shelia demanded.

''It's a subpoena, Mrs. Porter. Just a technicality. I'm sure you were planning on coming to the hearing anyway.''

''You can't subpoena me,'' Shelia shouted.

''Why, of course I can, Mrs. Porter. I need you to tell the judge that the gift was for you and that you and Mr. Porter had a perfect marriage. Basically just what you've told us here this evening.''

''But...''

Joanna paused in her trek toward the door. Gabe watched as she remained still, just the hint of a smile toying with the corners of her mouth. Luckily for the two of them, they had their backs to the Widow Porter. Gabe guessed the tall blonde wouldn't take too kindly to being snickered at.

''There won't be a problem,'' Joanna assured the woman. ''I'm sure the court will be impressed by your honesty. Bye.''

''She won't say any of that stuff in court,'' Gabe said while they waited for the elevator. ''And if she did, it wouldn't look too good for Rose.''

''Not true,'' Joanna said as she lifted her eyes to meet his. ''If Shelia sticks to her story about being the loving wife in the perfect marriage, I'll present evidence to the contrary. I'll show the court she's a liar and use whatever she says to ruin her credibility if Harris decides to call her for trial. If she changes her story, I have the tape of our interview. No matter what she says in court, she's just hung herself.''

Gabe smiled down at her. ''Nicely done.''

She gave him a playful jab in the ribs and said, ''Fifth in my class, remember?''

Chapter Six

"Will I be called to testify?" Lucy asked as she came up to where Joanna was standing with Rose in a quiet corner of the courthouse. The building smelled of stale coffee and bacon and there was a din of muffled conversations and staccato footsteps.

Joanna turned and regarded the young woman, amazed as usual by her appearance. Today she had on a dark wig, cat's-eye-shaped dark glasses and bloodred lipstick. A mole had been drawn low on her cheek, and her tailored suit was the same sable brown as her Jackie Kennedy teased bob. The only note of color on her was a brightly patterned scarf tied around her neck. She looked like something from the dawn of the television era.

"Probably," Joanna answered, still amazed by the transformation in the young woman. Apparently Lucy lived her life as if it were one continuous audition, complete with hair, makeup and posture appropriate for the character of the moment. "Please sit behind Rose when we go inside. I want everyone together so the judge gets to see the outpouring of support from her friends and family.''

"Sure thing," Lucy said as she reached out to give Rose a reassuring squeeze with one gloved hand.

"How do you manage to keep a straight face around your employees?" Joanna asked her client as soon as Lucy had walked over to join Susan, the Tanners and Rose's sons and their wives.

"Susan has been with me from the start," Rose answered. "She grows on you after a while. So long as you ignore all that crap about crystals and pyramids. Since Lucy started, business is up about seventeen percent. The customers get a kick out of her characters.''

"Listen, Rose," Joanna began carefully. "I need to tell you—"

"I just read the assignment board," Langston growled as he came to her side and grasped her arm, jerking her around so that they faced each other. "Have you told her?"

"I was just about to, when so rudely interrupted.''

"What are you two talking about?" Rose demanded.

"Your attorney has put you in a very precarious position," Gabe said.

"I'm going to ask him to recuse himself," Joanna said between clenched teeth. "And keep your voice down.''

"What is this all about?" Rose asked again.

Taking in a deep breath, Joanna turned to her client

and met her narrowed green eyes. "We drew Judge Halloran for the bail review. I'm going to make a motion that he not hear this case."

"Why?"

"Because Joanna sued the DA for sexual harassment three years ago and Halloran was the judge."

She glared up at Langston. "Will you stay out of this?"

"What does this mean?" Rose asked.

"It doesn't mean anything," Joanna said. "Except that it might cause a delay while they assign a different judge to the case."

"If they do——" Gabe said just loudly enough for Joanna to hear.

She was about to tell him to shut up, since his dire predictions were obviously shaking Rose's composure, but the courtroom doors opened and the bailiff called them inside.

"Don't worry," Joanna told Rose. She didn't say anything to Langston; she simply gave him a withering look that did little to erase the angry lines around his mouth and eyes.

The courtroom quickly filled with Rose's supporters and members of the local press. As she led Rose to her place at the defense table, Joanna felt a shiver of revulsion dance along her spine when the prosecutor and two of his assistants took their places.

"All rise."

Joanna clasped her hands in front of her as the

polished, robed judge climbed up to his perch at the front of the room.

As soon as Halloran took his seat, the room followed suit. The judge sat silently until the sounds of scuffing feet and shuffling papers quieted. He tapped his gavel once, then said, "Proceed," to the bailiff.

"State of South Carolina versus Rose B. Porter."

"Mr. Harris," the judge said as he gave the prosecutor a nod to begin.

Joanna was on her feet in an instant. "If it please the court, I have a motion that takes precedence over the state's request for a bail review."

Halloran met her eyes then. "Yes, Ms. Boudreaux?"

"While the defense has nothing but respect for Your Honor, I would point out that given the history of Your Honor, the prosecution and myself, it would be unfairly prejudicial to my client if you were to hear this matter."

He didn't move, she noted; not even an eyelash fluttered.

"The defense respectfully requests that Your Honor recuse himself and assign another judge to hear this case."

"Mr. Harris?" the judge asked.

"The prosecution feels that Your Honor is fully capable of hearing this case. To halt matters by appointing another judge would cause undue delay, as well as additional expense to the taxpayers."

The judge held up his hand, silencing Harris the Weasel.

"I anticipated this when I reviewed this matter."

Joanna held her breath.

"It is my opinion that should I remain sitting on this case, this defendant would have grounds for a mistrial based solely on the appearance of impropriety."

"But, Your Honor," Harris began to protest.

"I didn't say I liked it," Halloran sneered. "But in anticipation of Ms. Boudreaux's motion, I have already arranged for Judge Melinda Adams to hear this matter."

Joanna let out a relieved breath.

"It is therefore the order of this court that this matter be remanded to Judge Adams immediately."

"What does that mean?" Rose asked as she pulled at Joanna's jacket sleeve.

"It means we move one courtroom down with a new judge."

"Is that good or bad?" Rose asked anxiously.

Joanna was about to answer, when Don Harris sauntered over to their table. "Good morning, Joanna."

"Harris," she said as she began stuffing things into her briefcase.

"We can save ourselves some time if your client will agree to a plea. I'm prepared to—"

"What is he talking about?" Rose yelled.

Joanna placed her hand over Rose's and gave a

little squeeze. Then she turned to Harris and said, "My client isn't interested in a plea, Harris. She didn't do it."

Harris gave her a mirthless, superior smile. She longed to smack that expression off his face, but she knew that was exactly what he wanted.

"You might want to consider new counsel, Mrs. Porter," he said to Rose, even though his sharklike black eyes were fixed on Joanna. "Ms. Boudreaux has a personal agenda that might affect her judgment."

"Allow me to point out that it is a violation for you to speak to my client without my permission," Joanna said. "Keep it up and I'll be happy to file a complaint with the state bar."

Harris sighed almost contentedly. "You've tried that before, with rather disastrous results, as I recall."

"What the hell was that all about?" Rose demanded as soon as Harris had gone happily away.

"The DA and I don't share a mutual respect," Joanna answered as she closed her briefcase. "Don't worry. He's just blowing hot air."

"It didn't sound that way to me," Rose persisted. "I'm supposed to tell you everything, but you get to have secrets."

"It isn't important," Joanna said more forcefully. She met Rose's gaze. "Unless you're interested in a deal?"

Rose stiffened. "Hell, no! I didn't kill anyone."

"Then let's go."

"Where?"

"Judge Adams is waiting."

"UPON REVIEW of newly discovered evidence, the state believes Mrs. Porter is a threat to the community and therefore, bail should be revoked."

Joanna waited until Harris was seated before she stood with her hands steepled on top of the wooden table. "Mr. Harris failed to advise the court on several key points."

"I'm sure you'll set him straight," Judge Adams quipped.

This jurist was exactly the judge Joanna needed if she was going to win this case. Melinda Adams was known for her fairness and her feminist leanings. It didn't hurt that Joanna had clerked for her when she had first come to Charleston. Judge Adams was no-nonsense and considered by many in the legal community to be pro-defense. She had worked hard to attain her judgeship, and if anyone would keep Harris on a short leash, she would.

Joanna glanced once at her notes, then up to the salt-and-pepper-haired woman in the black robe. "Mrs. Porter's kidnapping conviction was nothing more than a custody dispute and it happened more than two decades ago. That is the real explanation of what Mr. Harris deemed a 'criminal history.' As to the state's claims that Mrs. Porter is a danger to the community, he said he based that on threats made to Mrs. Shelia Porter, the widow of the deceased. I have subpoenaed Shelia Porter for the purposes of clearing up this matter for the court.''

''Is that necessary?'' the judge asked.

Joanna looked over at Harris. ''Not if the prosecution is willing to stipulate that the pattern of harassment he referred to took place almost thirty years ago.''

Harris's face turned beet-red. Joanna felt a childish urge to stick her tongue out at him.

''Well?'' Judge Adams asked Harris.

The DA made a production out of talking to his assistant. Then he motioned to Shelia, who was seated directly behind the prosecutor's table, dressed in an expensive black-on-black outfit that flattered her willowy figure.

''She looks like something out of a bad gangster movie,'' Rose grumbled. ''The mob boss's trophy wife.''

''Shh,'' Joanna warned.

Harris got to his feet. ''The state is willing to stipulate that the harassment is somewhat removed from the murder of Mr. Porter. However, Mrs. Shelia Porter is fearful that the defendant poses a risk to her personal safety now that she is in Charleston.''

''Your Honor,'' Joanna began.

Judge Adams silenced her with a raised hand. ''There's no need, Ms. Boudreaux. I find no compelling reason to modify the order of the magistrate. Bail is continued for the defendant.'' Her gavel came down with a resounding thud. "How do you plan to proceed, Mr. Harris?"

"The state will hold a preliminary hearing at the court's earliest date."

Joanna felt herself frown. Why not just go to the grand jury? she wondered. A preliminary hearing took time and allowed a kind of preview into their case. It was far easier for the prosecutor to present his evidence in secret to the grand jury for an indictment. *In secret.* That was it. It was an election year and obviously Harris planned to use the Porter case to keep his name in front of the public. *What a slime,* she thought as she grabbed her calendar out of her briefcase.

"Very well," Judge Adams said. "We'll reconvene in this courtroom two weeks from Monday." The gavel fell again.

"What does all this mean?" Rose asked as soon as the judge had left the bench.

"It means Harris is giving us a chance to get the charges dismissed."

"That's good, right?" Rose asked with hope punctuating every word.

"It's scary," Joanna said as she regarded her client.

Rose had done exactly what she had asked in the way of clothing. The only trace of the real Rose was the necklace of large beads that she wore with her bland black-and-white dress. The spotted beads reminded Joanna of dalmatians.

"Harris wouldn't risk a dismissal unless he was

very sure of his case.'' Joanna brushed her bangs off to one side. ''There isn't anything you haven't told me, is there?''

She did it again, Joanna thought, when Rose lowered her eyes.

''No.''

''Good, because if I find out you've lied, you'll need a new lawyer.''

''I SHOULDN'T BE NERVOUS,'' Joanna told herself as she tried on yet another outfit. ''Who am I kidding?'' she asked her reflection. In the past ten days she had found herself growing more and more attracted to Gabriel Langston. It didn't help much that he had a habit of brushing against her, or allowing his fingers to linger just a fraction of a second when they exchanged documents or photos.

She finally settled on a pair of white walking shorts and a sleeveless pale-aqua knit shirt with a high neck. She braided her hair as she slipped into her sandals. The organizer in her purse chirped at the same time she heard the knock at her front door.

Grabbing her bag, she silenced the organizer as she went down the steps, hating herself for the feelings churning her stomach. They were going to Susan's for a follow-up interview. It wasn't a date, so why was she filled with more anticipation than a girl about to go to her prom?

He knocked again as she stood with her back

against the door, taking in a few deep, calming breaths.

Her effort to relax was wasted the instant she opened the door. He looked positively gorgeous standing there. His jeans fit snugly across powerful thighs and his pale rayon shirt wasn't completely buttoned, so she was treated to a glimpse of the dark hair covering the corded muscle of his broad chest. His hair was pulled back, enhancing his light eyes and deeply tanned skin. Once again, she couldn't find a single flaw.

"Ready?"

Ready, willing and able, she thought as she offered a simple nod. "I've just got to grab my briefcase out of the office."

"Take your time," he called after her.

As she hunted for her briefcase, Joanna repeated to herself all the valid reasons she shouldn't pursue anything with him.

"Damn," she muttered.

"Looking for this?"

Joanna spun around and felt the bow at the base of her neck flutter from the motion. He was in the doorway, one foot crossed over the other at the ankle, her briefcase in one hand, a sensual half smile on his face.

Things are getting way out of hand, she decided. Her pulse was erratic, her mouth was as dry as the proverbial bone, and all the man had done was smile. *Get control of your hormones!*

"Is something wrong?" he asked as he placed her

briefcase on one of the chairs and came around the desk.

"Nothing at all," she said in a helium-high voice that made her blush all the way to the roots of her hair.

He moved closer, his form completely filling her field of vision. The purely masculine scent of his cologne reached out to tease her just a second before his hand gently cupped the side of her face. With just the slightest pressure, he forced her head back, until she had no choice but to meet his piercing gaze. The gold that surrounded his pupils seemed to sparkle as he looked deeply into her eyes.

"Joanna." He said her name on a barely audible breath, making it sound like a plea.

When she lifted her hands and placed them on his chest, it had been with the full and rational intention of pushing him away. Good intentions sort of dropped by the wayside when she felt the muscle beneath her fingertips react to her touch. Her eyes dropped to her hands as she slowly ran the tips of her nails along the contours of hair and muscle, moving lower and lower, until she felt the succession of ropelike hard muscle that gave his stomach that washboard feel.

"I hope you're planning to finish what you're starting," he said as his hand snaked around her waist and pulled her against him.

There was no need for him to explain what he meant…she could feel him pressed against her belly. That knowledge brought her to her senses.

"I'm sorry," she stammered as she tried to step away from him. "Really, Langston, I shouldn't have done that." She looked up, expecting to have him scowling down at her. His brilliant smile was a total surprise. "I'm saying no," she said more forcefully.

"I know. I heard you."

"Then why are you smiling? And why won't you let me go?"

"Because," he murmured, "this is the first time you've given me any response. I'm just glad to know I haven't totally lost my touch."

His hand slid up in an achingly slow motion, until his fingers entwined in her braid. Gently he tugged until her head fell backward.

"Was I supposed to swoon at your feet, Langston?" Joanna teased.

"Not yet," he said as he lowered his mouth onto hers.

It wasn't a kiss. It was a seduction. He somehow managed to touch her all over, bombarding her with sensation as he teased her with his tongue and lips. It wasn't at all what she had expected, what she'd been bracing herself for almost from the beginning. There was no savagery, no impatience, no arrogance. This kiss was oddly subtle and passionate. The disciplined way he urged her mouth to open under his was something she catalogued in the major surprise area of her brain.

But when he deepened the kiss, her brain threatened to go on strike altogether. His other hand had moved to her waist, holding her still as he expertly tantalized her with only his mouth. The touch of his mouth was devastating in its simplicity and Joanna found herself nearly overcome by the urge to shove him down on the desk and rip his clothing off.

"Wait," she said against his mouth.

"That's what I've been doing," he said as he moved back and sat on the edge of her desk and drew her to stand inside his thighs.

In this position, she was almost eye to eye with him. Of course, she wished he'd picked someplace other than her desk, given her last wicked thought.

Joanna toyed with one of the buttons of his shirt, careful to keep her eyes averted. "Langston, I—"

"Since I've had my tongue down your throat, don't you think you should call me 'Gabe'?"

Not expecting the attack, Joanna started, her head coming up, and she was again surprised to see him grinning. "That was crude."

"It was the only thing I could think of to get you to look at me."

"You could have asked," she argued, horrified when the words came out in the sort of pout she would have expected from some bimbo on a one-night stand.

"You have a habit of doing the exact opposite of what I ask."

Joanna couldn't help smiling along with him. "I can be stubborn at times."

"But you're very beautiful when you smile."

"Don't do that," she requested as heat came flooding to her cheeks.

"You have a problem with a man telling you you're beautiful?"

"Only when the man saying it makes me look like a troll."

Gabe gave her a little shake. "What is that supposed to mean?"

Her lashes fluttered before she garnered enough nerve to meet his gaze. "You make me feel a little inadequate."

"Me?"

Joanna shook her head. "Men like you usually gravitate to the tall, leggy blondes with the boobs that arrive five minutes before they do."

His head fell back and he laughed. "I think your perception of me is a little off base."

"C'mon, Langston. Really attractive men always end up with superattractive women. Not short redheads with organizers and freckles."

"I happen to be partial to short redheads with freckles. The organizer is a bit of a pain."

"Funny," she acknowledged as she pretended to punch him in the gut. "But I'm serious. You are way out of my league."

"I'm in a league now?"

Joanna made a small disgusted sound. "You know perfectly well what I mean. Aside from the fact that you're 'drop-dead gorgeous,' to quote a friend, you've also got money coming out the wazoo. That's the big leagues, Langston.''

''Please stop doing that,'' he groaned. ''I haven't been called 'Langston' since my police days.''

''Speaking of which—'' Joanna paused for a fortifying breath, then looked into his eyes and asked ''—why did you leave the force?''

Gabe's expression grew dark, hard and almost scary. ''I killed an innocent man.''

Chapter Seven

"An accidental shooting?" Joanna asked.

Gabe fixed his eyes on a place over her head as he laced his fingers behind her back. The pain she read in his expression was almost palpable and she experienced a strong urge to comfort him.

"No, Phil was my partner."

"I'm sorry, Gabe," she said softly. "I know that accidents happen when—"

"It wasn't an accident."

Joanna stiffened, partly because of his curt tone and partly from shock. "What do you mean?"

"Phil's dead and it was my fault. Simple."

"How did it happen?"

He closed his eyes for a moment, and when he opened them he looked at her with a haunted expression. "Does it matter?"

"I think it does to you," she said softly as her hands moved to rest against him. She felt the even rise and fall of his chest as he breathed deeply. "Tell me about it."

"There's not much to tell."

"If you accidentally shot your partner—"

"I didn't pull the trigger, but his death was my fault all the same."

"What do you mean you didn't pull the trigger?"

Gabe blew out a long breath. "We were looking for this guy we thought had information about a narcotics shipment. Our snitch told us he was just a dealer, not the controlling party."

"So this dealer shot your partner?"

Gabe's head moved fractionally. "I told Phil to wait until I ran the dealer's street name. Phil was in a hurry, so he went in for the meet while I waited in the car for the dispatcher to patch me through to central."

"Why was Phil in such a hurry?" Joanna asked.

Gabe laughed sadly. "He had a date that night. He wanted to get the information and turn it over to the narcotics task force so he could call it a day."

"I don't understand why you think his death was your fault."

"I should have followed him in. That's one of the first things they teach at the academy. Instead I was sitting in the car, sipping coffee, while that scum blew his head off."

Joanna shivered at the image. In her two years with the DA's office, she'd seen more than enough shooting victims. They were never pretty.

She lifted her palm to his cheek and stroked the soft stubble of growth. "It doesn't sound to me like you could have done anything to prevent his death. If you'd gone in with him, you might very well have been killed, as well.''

"If I'd insisted Phil wait with me, he wouldn't be dead.''

"If I'd insisted my mother stop smoking, she wouldn't be dead, either,'' Joanna said.

"It isn't the same thing.''

Holding his gaze, she said, "Sure it is. I couldn't control my mother's behavior any more than you could control your partner's. That doesn't make either one of us responsible.''

"I could have prevented it.''

"Why? How? Just because you have the clarity of hindsight doesn't mean you would have acted differently at that time.''

Gabe stood and placed her away from him. "I appreciate what you're saying, but I'd really like to drop the subject.''

Joanna didn't want to drop it, but one look at him kept her silent.

On the drive to Susan's house, Joanna was quiet as she mulled over their conversation. It explained a lot. At least now she understood why Gabe was so stuck on protecting people. Obviously he was on a mission for some sort of personal redemption.

Gabe brought the Mercedes to a halt in the drive of a small home. There wasn't anything special about the house. And anyway, Joanna was more intrigued by the woman kneeling at the edge of the flower bed than she was the house.

As Lucy stood, she wiped her hands on a rag in one of the pockets of her blue gingham apron. She smiled brightly as she twisted the braids on either side of her face.

"She's good," Joanna said to Gabe as Lucy, complete with ruby slippers, walked across the small lawn to meet them.

"She's strange," Gabe grumbled. "Maybe she'll click her heels together three times and go back to Kansas."

"Hush," Joanna warned as she opened the car door. "I might need her as a character witness."

"'Character' being the operative word when it comes to Lucy McGuire."

"Good morning," Lucy said with a bright smile.

"Hi," Joanna returned, her eyes fixed on the other woman's face. "How long does it take you to do the makeup?"

Lucy might have blushed, but there was too much stage paint on her face to see her real skin tones. Shrugging modestly, she answered, "It depends on the character. Streisand takes the most time because I have to mold the nose out of latex."

"Hi!" Susan called from the now-open front door. "Come on in. I have tea ready."

Joanna and Gabe were silent as they entered the small house. The smell of incense was nearly overwhelming, as was the decor. The furnishings could only be described as eclectic. The sofa, chairs and tables were all draped with fabric. Crystals, pyramids and tarot cards were everywhere.

Susan ushered them into what Joanna guessed was the living room, though it was hard to tell from the decor what the purpose of the room actually might be.

"I've arranged chairs around the table," Susan said as she waved an arm with at least twenty bracelets in the direction of a small, round table with four chairs.

In the center of the table were two bowls. One bowl appeared to be filled with water; the other had a small amount of what looked like crushed leaves.

Lucy and Susan took their seats, which left Joanna and Gabe to sit side by side at the cramped setting. Susan seemed quite hyper, while Lucy appeared almost bored. Joanna glanced up to find a pyramid suspended by fishing line directly overhead.

"This shouldn't take too long," Joanna began.

"I need to prepare first," Susan said as she closed her eyes and her lips moved in some sort of silent incantation.

Joanna and Gabe exchanged looks as Susan began breathing so deeply that Joanna was afraid the woman would hyperventilate before she asked the first question.

"Okay," Susan said as her eyes opened. "It won't take but a minute for me to read the leaves."

"Read the leaves?" Joanna asked.

Susan bobbed her head. "I told you I had the tea all ready."

"Oooo-kay," Gabe said, obviously entertained by the strange woman.

Susan wasn't even phased by Gabe's apparent amusement at her expense. Using her fingertips, Susan drizzled some of the tea onto the water, then wrapped her hands around the ceramic bowl, again closing her eyes. This must not have been Lucy's first time because she, too, closed her eyes. This left Gabe and Joanna no choice but to look at each other. Gabe took his finger and made circles near his brain. Joanna quickly reached out and grabbed his hand, then mouthed the word "behave." The twinkle of laughter in his eyes didn't diminish one bit and Joanna found herself struggling to keep her composure as the tea ceremony continued. Susan asked for a sign from someone or something, then asked for clarity of memory. Gabe mouthed the words "nut case" in response. Joanna reached over and dug her nails into his leg.

Susan finally opened her eyes and stared into the bowl of soggy leaves. Her expression grew perplexed.

"Is something wrong?" Lucy asked.

"Just a lot of negative energy," Susan answered. "There's some real evil here."

Gabe leaned over and whispered in Joanna's ear. "Probably the spirit of the Lipton Tea Company ticked off because she's wasting perfectly good tea leaves."

Joanna bit her lip to keep from laughing. "Susan?"

she prodded when several more minutes went by with nothing happening but the weird waitress blowing the tea around the bowl. "I really do need to ask you some questions."

Susan looked up and nodded. "Let me get rid of these and put some vanilla in the oven. It won't take a minute."

"Vanilla what?" Gabe asked.

"Extract," Lucy replied with a healthy amount of tolerance. "Susan uses vanilla to keep in touch with the aura of her childhood."

"She's certifiable," Gabe murmured.

Lucy smiled. "Hey, it's harmless. But living here is never dull."

Joanna felt herself relax. "No, I don't think it would be. Have you and Susan been friends long?"

Lucy shook her head. "Actually, I'm just staying here until I can find my own place. Susan offered to let me use her spare room when I got the job at the Rose Tattoo."

"That was nice."

"She's really sweet," Lucy answered. "Even if she is a little strange at times."

"And dressing like Dorothy from the *Wizard of Oz* is not?"

Joanna could have kicked him. Lucy looked genuinely hurt by his barb. "Apologize, please."

"Sorry, I didn't mean any offense. I was just curious about your penchant for dressing in costumes with wigs and all the rest."

The hurt drained from Lucy's eyes. Eyes Joanna noticed were blue today. Obviously the girl used colored contacts to change her eye color to fit her character.

"I studied drama in college," Lucy explained. "Like most struggling actresses, I'm only tending bar until I get my big break."

"Don't most aspiring actresses go to New York?" Gabe inquired.

"Only if you're an aspiring actress with enough money to afford New York. I'll end up there eventually. Until then, I've done some dinner theater and I'll keep practicing and polishing."

"Sorry," Susan apologized as she returned to the table. Deep worry lines wrinkled her forehead as she took her seat. "Now, what did you want to ask me?"

Joanna pulled her briefcase up to the table and took out the recorder and her legal pad. "How long have you known Rose?"

"A little under four years," Susan answered as she reached for the crystal hanging on a chain around her neck and held it in a tight fist. "I kinda came with the place."

"What does that mean?" Gabe asked.

Susan smiled. "I worked there when it was the Rusty Nail. When Rose bought the place she kept me on."

"So you've worked for Rose and Shelby since the start," Joanna repeated.

"Not Shelby," Susan corrected. "She bought in

later, when she was pregnant with Chad. He's three now and you've never seen a cuter or more spoiled child than Chad Tanner. Of course, I think that's because of what Shelby and Dylan went through. Did you know that—"

"Earth to Susan," Gabe interrupted. "Please try to answer Jo's questions without going off on tangents."

Susan snapped her mouth closed and looked hurt.

"Gabe didn't mean to sound so harsh," Joanna explained with a bright smile. "We only have a few more days until the hearing, so I need to work quickly."

Susan seemed pacified by her explanation. Out of the corner of her eye, Joanna saw that Gabe was anything but. His irritation was evident in the rigidness of his posture and the hard set of his angular jaw. She was sorry she had let him talk her into bringing him along. In Joanna's opinion, Susan was only dangerous if she felt threatened by your aura; and Lucy's only apparent enemy was a theater critic. There was nothing here for him to protect her from.

"Can you tell me a little bit about Rose and Joe Don's relationship?" Joanna asked.

"Volatile," Susan answered.

Joanna cringed. "What do you mean by that?"

"I just mean that before Joe Don came back, Rose acted like she hated him. Then he shows up, and in a few days they're acting like newlyweds."

"So they didn't argue?" Joanna asked as hope surged through her.

"Like cats and dogs," Lucy chimed in. "Rose isn't one to hide her feelings."

Joanna decided any hope of using Susan to plant the seeds of reasonable doubt was fleeting at best.

Susan began to shake her head. "That's just the way she is. The only person Rose treats kindly is Shelby. And that's only because I think she feels indebted to Shelby for buying in to the business when she was really close to going under."

"What about her relationship with J.D. and Wesley?" Gabe asked.

Joanna turned her eyes on him. "I'm not going to put either one of them on the stand unless I absolutely have to. If I do that, I'd open the door to the kidnapping and harassment for Harris."

"Humor me," Gabe insisted.

"I don't think—"

"Susan?" Gabe interrupted yet again.

Joanna sat back and tossed her pen on the pad before angrily crossing her arms in front of her. She was furious at him for interrupting her interview, and as soon as they left she would make darned sure he knew it.

"Wesley was pretty open to a reconciliation with Rose. Probably because he's a shrink. J.D. took longer to forgive Rose and I know that hurt her. Tory was a big help there. She used to work at the Tattoo, did you know that?"

Gabe shook his head.

"She kinda forced J.D. to treat Rose like a mother, but it took some doing."

Joanna's anger was about to simmer over. Glancing at her watch, she decided it was time to put an end to Gabe's pointless questions. "This is all fabulously interesting, but I need to know about Rose's relationship with Joe Don."

Susan and Lucy seemed startled by Joanna's sarcastic tone. Gabe just seemed to accept it. Good, she thought. Maybe he'll get the hint that I'm mad.

"Did Rose ever do or say anything that led you to believe she wanted Joe Don dead?"

Lucy shifted uncomfortably in her seat and Susan wore the expression of a child caught with her hand in the candy dish.

"I need to find out before the hearing," Joanna explained. "If you know something, tell me now so I can deal with it beforehand."

"Go ahead," Lucy said to Susan as she put her hand on the other woman's arm. "If you don't tell her now and the DA finds out, it will look bad for Rose."

Joanna sucked in a deep breath and held it. In the past few days Gabe had almost gotten her to believe that she was actually defending an innocent woman, in spite of the overwhelming evidence to the contrary. "What is it?"

Susan looked on the verge of tears. "It's about the necklace they found with his body."

"Was it for Shelia?" Joanna asked.

Susan shook her head. "No."

Joanna brightened somewhat. "Then it was a gift for Rose."

Susan's moist eyes met hers, then she slowly shook her head as her lower lip began to tremble. "It wasn't for Rose, either."

"For you?" Joanna asked.

Susan shook her head more vehemently. "It was for his other girlfriend."

"Joe Don had a girlfriend?" Gabe asked.

Chapter Eight

"Great," Joanna fumed. "You almost had me convinced that Rose was innocent."

Gabe clutched the steering wheel. "Just because Susan knew Joe Don had a girlfriend doesn't mean Rose knew anything about it."

"Right," she snorted. "The only way to prove that is to find the girlfriend."

"I'll find her," he said as he made the turn into the alley adjacent to the Rose Tattoo.

He followed Joanna through the back door of the building. Several of the kitchen workers watched them with unfettered curiosity as he trailed the petite redhead up the staircase.

Joanna pushed through the office door and he wasn't far behind. He entered just in time to see the surprise on Rose's face. Shelby was at her desk, holding Cassidy, who had a death grip on a ratty piece of blanket. Chad was on the floor, coloring on a piece of paper that now looked remarkably like something Warhol might have sold for a few hundred grand.

"I think you'd better take the kids downstairs," he said to Shelby.

The brunette looked from him to Joanna's taut, angry face and nodded. She shifted Cassidy to her hip as she stood. "Bring your crayons downstairs with us," she said to her son.

"I don't wanna," he wailed.

Gabe knelt next to the boy and gave him a bright smile. "How are you today, Chad?"

"Good," he said as he scraped a brown crayon in an arc above an oval-shaped blob. "I'm colorin'."

"Color*ing*," Shelby corrected. "Come on, Chad. Gabe and Aunt Rose need to have a private talk."

The small boy raised his wide blue eyes to his mother and asked, "Like when you and Daddy lock your door?"

Shelby turned a brilliant shade of crimson as she hurriedly took her offspring out of the room.

"So what are you doing here on a Sunday morning?" Rose asked.

Gabe moved over to the credenza so that he could see both women clearly. It was instantly apparent that Joanna had lost none of her anger. She stood with her legs slightly apart and her small hands balled into fists at her sides. Her briefcase lay abandoned by her feet and her eyes burned like the ocean reflecting the summer sun.

"When were you going to tell me about the girlfriend?" Joanna asked without preamble.

"What girlfriend?" Rose countered in an equally forceful tone.

"I got copies of the crime-scene photos," Joanna explained. "Joe Don was holding a wrapped gift in his hand when he was killed."

"What kind of gift?" Rose fired back. "And why are you yelling at me?"

"Because I've known for some time that you were hiding something from me. I can only conclude that Joe Don's girlfriend was the secret."

Rose ran her fingers along the strand of large glass beads that matched her fuchsia-and-green print blouse. "If he had a gift, it had to be for me," she said with confidence. "Joe Don wasn't seeing anyone."

"Susan says differently."

Gabe watched as Rose's face registered shock. His gut told him it wasn't an act. "You didn't know," he concluded softly. "Did you?"

"Stay out of this," Joanna hissed at him.

"I swear, I didn't know anything about it." Rose's eyes filled with sadness. "Are you sure?"

He heard Joanna let out a breath before she began pacing. "There's no way Harris will believe Susan knew about the girlfriend and you didn't. Showing motive will be a piece of cake once he introduces the gold chain."

"There was a gold chain in the box?" Rose asked.

"Yes," Joanna answered automatically.

Gabe scratched his head and asked, "Did Joe Don ever mention a woman to you?"

"Besides the coed?" Rose retorted with open hostility. "Not that I remember."

"Think," Joanna barked. "We have to get to this woman before Harris does, assuming he doesn't already know. Wait." Joanna dug into her briefcase and yanked out a sheet of paper. "This is Harris's witness list for the preliminary hearing. Any names you don't recognize?"

Rose took the list and inspected it. "I know everyone, except for this one, sort of."

"What is that supposed to mean?" Joanna asked as she moved to stand behind Rose to see which name she was pointing to.

"It means I know the name, but I've never actually met the woman."

"'Michelle Danforth,'" Joanna read aloud. "Who is she?"

"The sister of the man who was going to finance Joe Don's new company."

"Thanks," Gabe said, "I'll check her out."

"No," Joanna told him. "*We'll* check her out." She moved so that she was facing Rose across the desk.

The two women seemed to glare at each other, before Joanna said, "If I find out that you're not being totally honest with me, I'll immediately make a motion to have new counsel appointed."

"Jo," Gabe began, in the hope that he could calm

her temper. "Rose hasn't lied to you. She wouldn't do that. Right, Rose?"

"Of course not."

Gabe tried not to notice the slight hesitation in her voice when she gave her answer. He tried, but for the first time he found himself wondering if Rose could actually be guilty.

"I THINK we're barking up the wrong tree."

"I'm not really interested in what you think," Joanna said as she moved closer to the car door in an attempt to distance herself from him. "I'm not sure you're thinking straight if your behavior back at the Rose Tattoo was any indication."

"What behavior?"

She rolled her eyes and prayed for patience. "For whatever inane reason, you seem to wear a huge pair of blinders where Rose is concerned."

"I have faith in her innocence," he countered. "Haven't you ever believed one of your clients?"

"Sure. I believe they're guilty."

She could almost feel the animosity emanating from his large frame. It didn't matter, though; his blind faith in Rose's professed innocence grated on her nerves. She needed an investigator, not some guy who was unwilling or unable to look at the situation objectively.

"How did you get so cynical?" he challenged.

"I'm not cynical. I'm realistic."

"Rose could never kill Joe Don."

"How can you be so sure?" she demanded. "It makes absolutely no sense that you would feel that way. I'm sure when you were on the force you developed a cop's sense about people."

"That's how I know Rose isn't guilty."

"Unfortunately I can't call you *or* your gut instinct as a witness."

"Then hear me out," he suggested.

"Why?"

"Because you like the way I kissed you."

"It was okay."

Gabe suddenly veered the car to a stop at the curb. Releasing her seat belt, he took her by the arms and pulled her across the console. His mouth was on hers in a flash. It wasn't like the first time. It was even better. There was something terribly erotic about the controlled way he toyed with first her upper lip, then her bottom lip, before tasting the seam of her mouth.

When he finally released her, Joanna found herself breathless and her anger lost in the overwhelming rush of desire. As she moved back into her own seat, she struggled to get her pulse back to normal.

"Still think I'm just okay?" he asked smugly.

"Maybe a little better than okay," she reluctantly admitted as she buckled her seat belt.

"I'd be happy to kiss you again."

"No, thanks."

Gabe reached out and caught her chin, forcing her to turn and meet his gaze. "Are you going to pretend that you're immune to being kissed?"

That little flutter in her stomach refused to stop, especially when her eyes dropped to his mouth and the memory of the warmth and finesse of his kisses played in her mind.

"I'm just saying that this isn't the right time for us to..."

"Because it isn't in your organizer?" he teased.

"Something like that," she grumbled as she turned her head and studied her slightly trembling hands.

"So what do I have to do to get a listing in that thing?"

"This is a pointless conversation," Joanna told him. "I think you only started all this to distract me from discussing your lack of professional objectivity where Rose is concerned."

"Believing in Rose hardly means I've lost my objectivity."

"Then why did you ask Susan all those irrelevant questions about Rose and her sons?"

"Just getting background."

"The sons weren't in town when Joe Don was killed. And given their history with Rose, I have no intention of calling them as witnesses."

"Don't you wonder why she allowed him to take her children?"

"Not particularly," Joanna admitted. "It was a long time ago, and after meeting Wesley and J.D., neither of them seems emotionally shattered to me."

"Maybe she couldn't afford to keep them."

"This is a perfect example of what I've been telling

you," Joanna said as he put the car in gear and pulled back onto the road. "We've got the girlfriend to check out and all you seem interested in is Rose's less-than-relevant past."

She watched his expression grow hard, his eyes distant, as he tightened his grip on the wheel. It was hard to reconcile this stony person with the man who had the uncanny ability to kiss her into stupidity.

"Then how about this," he began tersely. "I think this girlfriend thing is a waste of time."

"How can you say that?"

"Because Susan is such a space cadet, I don't think we should be taking her suppositions to heart. For all we know, she came to the conclusion that Joe Don had a girlfriend because it came to her in a dream."

"So she's not the most grounded person I've ever met."

"Between Susan and the bartender with a thousand faces, I think we're doing nothing but chasing our proverbial tails."

"What do you suggest?"

Gabe took a deep breath and said, "I think we should focus on finding out every move Joe Don made since he arrived from Florida."

"In four days?"

"What's the most common reason for murder?"

"Money," she conceded.

"Right. So who gains from Joe Don's untimely demise?"

"Shelia, J.D. and Wesley, I guess."

"Right, Rose has nothing to gain."

"That we know of," Joanna reminded him. "And the second most popular motive for murder is a past and/or present relationship between the victim and the perpetrator. In fact, at Rose's and Joe Don's age and income bracket, I think crimes of passion are more common than financial motives."

"Well, the only motive we've uncovered for Rose so far is that she knew about Joe Don's extracurricular activities."

"We'll find out in just a few minutes."

Michelle Danforth lived in a posh development on the banks of the Cooper River. The three-story condos were large and rather pricey, compared with most of the other homes in the area. Joanna and Gabe were met by a uniformed guard at the gated entrance.

"May I help you?"

Joanna pulled out one of her business cards and passed it to Gabe to give to the elderly man. "We'd like to see Mrs. Danforth."

The guard bent down, his hands on Gabe's door as he gave her a strange look.

"Michelle Danforth?" Joanna said.

She could see the light dawn in his faded brown eyes. "That would be *Miss* Danforth," he explained in a cultured Southern drawl.

"Whatever," Gabe said impatiently.

The guard seemed to take offense at Gabe's remark. His shoulders drew back and the polite smile fell away from his mouth.

"Please wait here while I see if Miss Danforth is available."

"Nice going, Gabe. Very smooth. Why don't you tell him he looks like a fool in that uniform?"

"I hate being held up by rent-a-cops."

"Gee, isn't that what *you* are these days?" Joanna asked with a mocking smile.

Gabe looked down at her and matched her snide expression. "You know what I mean."

"All I know is that you annoyed that guy, which could—"

"Miss Danforth will see you," the guard said as soon as he emerged from the gatehouse. "Park over there and follow this walkway to the end, take a left, and she's on the third floor of the next-to-last building."

"I wonder what Miss Danforth does," Gabe said a few minutes later as they walked along the perfectly laid brick walk lined with flowering shrubs. "This place is all individual ownership."

"How do you know that?"

"I looked here when I first came to Charleston."

"But you didn't buy? I'd live here in a heartbeat."

"No, you wouldn't. They have a list of rules and regulations a mile long. You can only use a certain type of furniture on the balconies. All draperies must be lined with white fabric. I felt like I was joining the military, not buying a house."

"So where did you end up?"

"I have a little place out at the beach."

"Would I think it was little?"

"There's only one way to find out."

"Pictures?"

He grinned at her. "You can come out for dinner tonight."

"I don't think—"

"I didn't ask you to think. I asked you over for dinner."

"That's the problem," she said under her breath.

"This is it." Gabe grabbed her arm just as she reached the front door. "We don't talk to Miss Danforth until you agree to have dinner with me."

Joanna gave a futile tug of her arm. "You're being childish again, Langston."

"I thought we agreed that you would use my given name. Now, agree to have dinner with me."

Joanna looked up and met his eyes. "Just so there's no misunderstanding, I'm willing to have dinner with you, but that's it."

"Do you negotiate *everything?*"

"I'm a lawyer," she reminded him. "I thrive on negotiating."

"Fine. Then we're on for dinner and anything else is negotiable."

"But—"

Gabe placed his finger to her lips. "Hush, Jo. You'll have fun. I promise. Now, come on. We don't want to keep Miss Danforth waiting."

Joanna wasn't sure whether to be flattered or annoyed. Intellectually, she knew she should tell him to take a hike. However, someplace in the secret recesses of her mind, she also acknowledged that he was an interesting, if somewhat overbearing, man. He was also the first man she could remember who actually made her palms sweat.

"Very nice," Joanna said as they stepped off the elevator onto very soft, lush carpeting. The hallways were professionally decorated, with interesting artwork and well-cared-for potted plants. They found Michelle Danforth's condo by following a series of arrows posted discreetly on the wall. Gabe pressed the doorbell.

The woman who greeted them was not at all what Joanna had expected. Joe Don had been nearly sixty, yet this woman appeared young enough to be studying for her SATs.

"You must be the attorney Mr. Harris spoke of," she said on a rush of air.

Her voice was so breathy that Joanna felt certain the woman could always find work as a phone-sex operator, should she fall on hard times. Of course, her observation could have something to do with the way Michelle looped her diamond-dripping arm around Gabe as she ushered him into the condo. Joanna was left to close the door and lug her briefcase. She did so, all the while studying the way the leggy brunette seemed to float as she walked. She had a dancer's body, complete with a neat bun and a graceful neck. The dress she had chosen would have looked plain on just about anyone else. On this woman, the simple linen garment with the scooped neckline and formfitting shape was like a tribute in red to less than three percent total body fat.

"Mr. Harris mentioned you might be paying me a visit," Michelle said as she draped her long body in a chair. "He also told me that I am under no obligation to talk to you."

"That's correct," Joanna said, glad that her catty thoughts hadn't been betrayed by her tone. She pulled the tape recorder and a legal pad from her briefcase and dug a pen out of her purse. "I do appreciate the fact that you are willing to speak to me."

"Thank your attractive friend here," Michelle replied boldly.

Joanna stifled the urge to stick her finger down her throat and barf all over the woman. "This is Mr. Langston. He's a private detective."

Michelle fairly purred as she moved over to the love seat and arranged herself next to Gabe. Actually, Joanna thought, Michelle was as next to him as she could get without technically being in his lap.

Michelle reached out and traced one of the buttons of Gabe's shirt. "Do you do all the dangerous work, Mr. Langston?"

"My friends call me 'Gabe,'" he said in a tone full of male ego.

"Gabe," Michelle repeated.

"Gag," Joanna mumbled. "If you don't mind, I would like to talk to you about Mr. Porter."

Michelle's full lower lip jutted out in a classic, if

not comical, pout. "I just hate it that Joey got himself killed. It's so…violent."

"Death usually is," Joanna said dryly. "Would you mind telling me what your relationship to—*Joey*—was?"

Michelle turned her large brown eyes on Joanna, and as casually as she might comment on a nicely appointed room she said, "We had sex together."

Joanna swallowed. Gabe's expression was bland. Michelle seemed to have enjoyed her own bluntness.

"Joey and my brother have some business dealings. Speaking of which," Michelle stopped talking, arched her back and managed to place her arm around Gabe's shoulder in one fluid motion.

Joanna had to bite her tongue to keep from asking the woman how much she had paid for her breasts. Too catty, too unprofessional, too childish. But it would have felt good.

Michelle continued, "Are you Gabe Langston of Langston Publishing?"

"I was," Gabe told her. "I sold the company a few months back."

"I'd be happy to give the two of you an opportunity to discuss idle riches later. For now, could we just get through a few questions?"

"Joanna gets a little testy at times," Gabe explained to Michelle. "Let's humor her."

"Let's," Joanna agreed as she felt every muscle in her body tense. "How long had you and *Joey* been…intimate?"

"Intimate," Michelle repeated with a little laugh.

"I'm sorry," Joanna said with a sweet smile. "Does that word have too many syllables in it for you?"

Michelle's pleasant, carefree expression turned venomous as she glared at Joanna. "Ouch," she said with a sigh. Then, lifting her arm so that her hand was free, she coiled Gabe's hair around her finger. "Have I wandered into another woman's territory?"

"Don't be silly," Joanna replied with a nervous laugh. "Sorry about that last remark. It was uncalled for. However, I would like to know how long you and Mr. Porter had been seeing each other."

"About three months," Michelle answered. "I met him at the juice bar at my gym. He seemed like a nice guy. Things just progressed from there."

"Did he ever mention his wife?"

"Do you mean Shelia or Rose?"

"Both, either."

"He told me he had left Shelia—his current wife—about six months before we met. He said he was reestablishing his ties with Rose while we were together."

"And that didn't bother you?" Joanna asked.

Michelle gave a throaty little laugh. "Lord, no. I like men like Joey—no ties, no conditions, just sex."

"A little dangerous in this day and age."

"We were always careful…especially since I knew of at least one other."

"One other what?" Joanna asked.

"One other woman in Joey's life."

Chapter Nine

"What other woman?" Joanna asked.

Michelle waved her hand—the one that wasn't toying with Gabe's hair—dismissively in the air. "It would have been gauche of me to ask," she said. "But I did overhear a portion of a telephone conversation. Which is what seemed to excite Mr. Harris."

"What did you hear?" Gabe asked.

"I wasn't intentionally eavesdropping, mind you."

"Of course not," Joanna agreed sweetly.

"And all I heard was the last part of the conversation."

"What did you hear?" Gabe delivered the question as a sort of soft command.

Michelle seemed somewhat amused by his small display of temper. She probably liked to be tied up and spanked, Joanna thought. Yep, Michelle Danforth was nothing but a spoiled, snooty woman completely lacking in any moral fiber. Of course, the fact that Michelle was beautiful, self-confident and obviously quite comfortable with her relationships with men had nothing to do with the harshness of her assessment. *Yeah, right.*

"Did Mr. Porter ever talk about this other woman, maybe tell you her name?"

Michelle shook her head. "No name other than Rose. And from the snippet of conversation I overheard, I assumed he was talking to her."

"Why would you assume that?" Gabe asked.

"Because I met Rose," Michelle answered.

"Rose said she had never met you."

"Well, we didn't actually meet. I saw her with Joey, and when I overheard the conversation it made me think of her. Incidentally, the woman has absolutely no sense of style," Michelle said with a look of complete distaste. It was as if simply thinking of Rose's loud clothing had left a bad taste in her mouth.

"I still don't follow," Joanna prompted. "Why did you think Joe Don was talking to Rose?"

"Because he told her to wear something exotic. She's the only woman I've ever seen who looks like a walking safari, so…"

"YOU MISSED the turn," Joanna said. It was the first time she had spoken since they had left Michelle's condo.

"No, I didn't," Gabe answered. "We're going to my place."

She felt a knot of tension in her stomach. "Are you sure that will be all right with Michelle?" Joanna said the woman's name by mimicking her breathy tone.

Gabe chuckled. "Jealous?"

"Hardly. I just think it was a little crass of her to write her number on a piece of paper and then shove it into your front pocket. It also doesn't take that long to pass a note," Joanna said.

"So she's a little on the brazen side," Gabe admitted. "I'll bet she doesn't use an organizer."

"I'll bet her bedroom is full of whips, chains and other adult paraphernalia."

"You didn't like her," Gabe remarked.

Resting her head against the seat, she closed her eyes. "I doubt a jury will, either."

"Unless the jury is all male."

She wanted to punch him. "Fortunately for me, the hearing will be before Judge Adams, and I doubt she'll be overly impressed by that walking tribute to plastic surgery."

"I agree."

"You could have fooled me," Joanna huffed. "The woman was all over you."

Gabe turned his head for a second and looked at her. "Is there a reason you found that so bothersome? Is it possible that you like me?"

"Don't flatter yourself. I'm annoyed because I don't like the type of woman Michelle Danforth represents."

"Which is?"

"Rich, spoiled and completely without conscience."

"How do you know she's without conscience?"

"Because she didn't care that Joe Don was sleeping with her while he was seeing Rose."

"And that bothers you?"

"Call me old-fashioned," Joanna said, "but I have fairly strong views on monogamous relationships."

"Is that why you turned Harris in?"

"Do we really have to discuss this?" Just as Joanna asked the question, the flashing red light came on ahead of them, indicating that they would have to wait for the drawbridge.

Gabe was obviously accustomed to it, because he stopped the Mercedes and cut the engine. That done, he unfastened his seat belt and shifted his large frame so that he almost faced her. Joanna turned away, pretending to watch the masts of the three sailboats lined up and waiting below in the river.

"Jo?" he prompted.

"There isn't much to tell," she hedged. "Harris is a dirtbag and I was a young, idealistic assistant DA."

"That doesn't explain why Harris tried to have you disbarred."

"He did that out of spite and a need to save face with his wife and the community."

"But it doesn't tell me what happened."

Slowly, she turned her head and met his probing eyes. "Do you want all the gory details, or will a summary of the high points do?"

He seemed genuinely hurt by her sarcasm. His hand came to rest on her bared knee and he gave her leg a small squeeze that was nearly her undoing.

"I'd like to hear whatever you want to tell me."

Joanna lowered her gaze, knowing it would be easier if she wasn't looking at him as she told the story. "I had just finished clerking for Judge Adams, when Harris offered me a job with his office. I was thrilled, since I knew I didn't want to spend my career doing civil work."

"And you wanted to get the bad guys?"

Joanna smiled in spite of the lingering pain these memories inspired. "I guess so. I liked being on the right side of justice and I worked my tail off."

"Which impressed Harris."

Joanna shrugged. "Looking back, I'm not sure he even took any notice of what I was doing in the courtroom. When he asked me to be second chair for the Binghampton murder case, I was understandably elated. It was a complicated murder case, with four codefendants all scrambling to incriminate the others in the hope of making a deal." Joanna looked out the car window again, fixing her eyes on the odd blend of expensive homes and shacks that lined the riverbank. "I believed Harris when he told me his wife had died. He claimed he had loved her so much that he couldn't stand to remove her photos from his office or take off his wedding band. He was charming and said all the things I wanted to hear."

"Not an uncommon thing for men who cheat on their wives."

"It only happened once," Joanna said, unable to get her voice above a barely audible whisper. "The very next day I just happened to be in his secretary's office, when his wife called."

"That must have been a shock."

Joanna shrugged. "I think someplace in my mind I knew he'd been lying to me from the word go. I just didn't choose to acknowledge the obvious."

"Did you love him?"

"I respected him and I was lonely. My father had just passed away and maybe I was using Harris as much as he was using me."

"Then why the lawsuit?"

Joanna sighed. "Harris didn't take it very well when I called him a lying pig and refused to 'overlook'—his word—the fact that his wife was alive and well."

"I take it he didn't back off?"

"He demoted me to trying misdemeanor traffic violations, then put me in night court for arraignments."

"I'm beginning to understand why you made the charge of harassment."

"I should never have done that."

Gabe squeezed her leg again before saying, "It doesn't sound like you had any choice."

"I should have just quit."

"But you knew Harris would probably do the same thing to the next young, attractive assistant who came along."

"So much for ideals," Joanna answered. "Harris and his attorney were able to pull all the e-mails off the computer, even though I had deleted them. By the time we went to trial, they made it look and sound as if I had been the one pursuing Harris, and that he only had me transferred to save himself from my 'fatal attraction'—again his words—''

"I don't think I'm going to like Harris very much."

That made her smile. "I accepted the outcome of the trial, but I was furious when he lodged a complaint with the bar association. He very nearly got my license to practice law suspended."

"I'm glad for Rose's sake that he failed."

"But the damage was done," Joanna told him. "I couldn't get a job as a prosecutor with any of the other counties. So I ended up making a living defending the same people I would have happily prosecuted."

Gabe started the engine as soon as the bells began to sound and the red-and-white striped barrier began to rise. "At least now I know why your heart isn't in what you do."

"That's not fair," Joanna protested as she looked at his profile. "I've done a good job and I've treated all my clients fairly."

"But you've never believed in their innocence, have you?"

"Because they usually aren't innocent."

"Well, Jo, Rose will be the exception. Harris will be the one chasing ambulances when he loses the election because he tried the wrong person for murder.''

She had to laugh. ''That would be something I would pay to see.''

Gabe turned down Bohicket Road and Joanna watched him out of the corner of her eye. The shadows cast by the branches of live oaks draped with Spanish moss danced with the fading sunlight. ''Where exactly is your little place at the beach?''

''Kiawah Island.''

Joanna stifled a groan. ''There isn't a little house on that whole island.''

''Compared with The Hamptons or Newport, it's—''

''Sorry, but I've never been to Newport or The Hamptons.''

''I'd be happy to arrange a trip after you get Rose acquitted.''

''Safe bribe,'' Joanna mumbled as he made the left into the popular resort community. Gabe was waved through by a guard. It seemed to Joanna that the farther they drove, the bigger the houses became. The parkway was lined with manicured ornamental shrubbery and tall, straight palm trees. Every now and then she could catch a glimpse of the paved bike path that ran parallel to the road. It was like being in another part of the state, she thought as they passed stately home after stately home. It didn't seem possible that they were less than twenty miles from downtown Charleston.

"This is your idea of a little beach house?" she asked when Gabe pulled into a horseshoe-shaped drive in front of an impressive two-story home complete with giant white columns and huge windows that revealed a massive carved staircase in the center of the house.

"Quiet," Gabe warned as he reached up to his sun visor and pressed something that made the garage open.

"My whole house would probably fit in here," Joanna said as he brought the car to a stop next to another vehicle, which was covered by a brown custom canvas. "What's under the tarp?"

"My other car," he answered with a bit of annoyance, or perhaps it was embarrassment, creeping into his tone.

"Other car," Joanna repeated with a smile. "Is this your other house, too?"

"Don't push, Jo," he warned softly. "And don't expect any apologies."

"I wouldn't dream of it," she insisted as she got out of the car. She followed behind him, unable to keep her tongue. "You know there are children starving in Ethiopia."

"Joanna!" was his stern reply.

"Just mentioning it," she claimed as she drew her lip between her teeth to keep from giggling.

"This is incredible," she gushed as soon as they entered the kitchen. "It looks like the set of one of those cooking shows." The long, galley-shaped kitchen came complete with a center island, over which hung copper pots, pans and lids in varying shapes and sizes. The cabinets had white trim and glass fronts. There was even a cabinet in the shape of a wine rack and it held several bottles of what she theorized were expensive vintages. The kitchen led into a dining area with one wall of floor-to-ceiling glass. She whistled when she looked out at the unobstructed view of the Atlantic Ocean. "That's breathtaking," she said without realizing she had spoken aloud.

"It's a nice view for morning coffee."

Joanna froze, trying to decide if that was his way of telling her he expected her to spend the night. He must have sensed her sudden apprehension, because he gave her a patient smile as he leaned against the hand-painted tile counter.

"That wasn't a come-on," he assured her. "I was merely agreeing with you."

Joanna relaxed.

"But I won't say no if you decide to stay and play house with me."

"HE'S HERE!" Tammy called from her desk. "I swear, it should be illegal for a man to be that handsome."

"I know," Joanna told her secretary.

"So—" Tammy paused long enough to blow a bubble with her gum "—why aren't you sleeping with him?"

Joanna rolled her eyes. "We don't have that kind of a relationship."

"If you don't, can I?"

"Hush," Joanna snapped.

Tammy smiled. "You say you aren't attracted and yet you totally freak out when someone else is. Is it possible that you're actually interested in him?"

"Don't be silly."

"He's interested in you," Tammy said with a wicked twinkle in her eyes.

"Not likely," Joanna countered. Tammy had no way of knowing that Joanna had insisted on being taken home immediately following their dinner the previous evening. Gabe hadn't even acted disappointed.

"I've seen the way he watches you when you aren't looking."

"Tammy," Joanna warned. "Give it a rest."

She had just finished delivering that edict, when Gabe came through the door. Joanna marveled at how refreshed and relaxed he appeared. It annoyed her slightly. Thanks to the bone-melting kiss he'd given her at the end of the evening, she had hoped he had suffered all night just as she had. But obviously it hadn't phased him.

"'Morning, ladies," he said through a wide smile.

Tammy looked as though she might swoon, but instead the secretary simply gave a small, grateful sigh. "You have things to do," Joanna reminded her.

Then, turning to go back into her office, she said, "So do I."

"Did you get up on the wrong side of the bed?" Gabe asked as he fell into the chair across from her.

"I just have a lot to do before the hearing," Joanna insisted. "Harris messengered over a stack of witness statements early this morning."

"Anyone you haven't talked to?"

"Michelle's brother, Peter Danforth. Rose's landlady, some guy named Mitch Fallon, and about five others. There's no way I can interview all these people in only three days *and* prepare Rose for the hearing."

"I'll help you," he offered.

"Thanks, but I think I have to read through them."

"I think we should go to Joe Don's apartment."

Joanna stared at him. "And why do you think we should do that, when I have about three hundred pages of statements to wade through?"

"Because we have to find out what Joe Don was into if we're going to find the real killer."

Joanna shook her head. "My job isn't to find the killer. My job is to defend Rose. I can't adequately prepare a defense if I don't know what Harris knows."

Gabe's expression grew hard. "Forget Harris, Jo. We need to know what Joe Don knew. Grab your purse."

"Grab my purse?" she parroted. "As in I'm just

supposed to drop everything and jump when you say jump?''

Gabe's brow wrinkled into a definite frown. ''Don't be difficult, Jo.''

''Don't treat me like a flunky,'' she countered. ''You work for me, remember? I call the shots—you don't.''

Gabe rose, picked up the recently delivered box full of witness statements and started to leave.

''What are you doing?''

''If you want to read these, I suggest you come with me.''

''You're acting childish again, Langston.''

''Just doing my job,'' he called over his shoulder.

Joanna wished she had a paperweight or something equally heavy that she could throw at his arrogant head. Furiously, she watched as Tammy scrambled to hold the door open for him.

Snatching her purse off the back of her chair, Joanna jogged after him, stopping only long enough to call Tammy a traitor. Gabe was loading the box into the trunk of his car when Joanna reached him. ''You're fired.''

''No, I'm not.''

Joanna wanted to scream. Gabe was relaxed, so much so that he was whistling when he came around to open the door for her. When she refused to budge, he took his sunglasses off the belt loop of his jeans and began to polish them with the tail of his shirt. He placed them on the tip of his nose and regarded her over the tops of the lenses.

"You're wasting time."

"You're an overbearing jerk."

"Get in the car, Jo."

"Be reasonable," she argued. "If you really want me to beat Harris, this isn't the way to do it. I have to be prepared."

"No," he said forcefully, "we have to find the real killer. That's the only way you'll be sure to beat Harris."

Whipping the strap of her purse over her head, Joanna glared up at him. "Thanks for the vote of confidence."

"Are you going to pout the whole trip?" Gabe asked after they had gone several miles in stony silence.

"I'm not pouting. I'm simmering."

"Are you mad because I made you come along or because I didn't make you stay with me last night?"

"Now I know why you live in that monstrous house. It's the only place you can fit your gargantuan ego."

"Calm down, Jo. This won't take long, and then I'll give you back your box and you can spend the whole night reading."

"Gee, thanks."

"You're welcome," he mimicked.

It was charitable to call the place Joe Don lived a home. The rooms he rented were in a dilapidated house in one of the parts of Charleston kept secret from the tourists. There were no historic markers, no fancy courtyards or bubbling fountains, only peeling siding and roofs patched with plastic trash bags.

Joanna watched the cracked walkway as she followed Gabe through an alley that wreaked of rotting garbage. Several pairs of eyes peeked through tattered window coverings as they climbed the rickety stairs to the second floor.

"What are you doing?" Joanna gasped.

"Picking the lock," Gabe answered casually.

"This is breaking and entering," she said as she wrapped her fingers around his wrist.

There was a faint click, then he threw the door open. "I didn't break a thing," he breathed. "And I don't think Joe Don will put up much of a fuss about trespassing."

"But I could have gotten permission for us to be here," Joanna argued as she remained on the threshold.

"It would take at least two days for your request to be processed by the police. You're the one who keeps harping on the fact that we only have three days before the hearing."

"I can lose my license for this," she hissed. "We could both face prosecution and Harris would love that."

Gabe turned and gave her an impatient look before grabbing her hand and yanking her inside. "No one will know," he said with amazing confidence.

"And you know this because?"

"Because the police have already been here and done their thing. By this afternoon Shelia, as his next of kin, will be able to come in here and take what she likes."

"So?"

Gabe dropped her hand and took hold of her shoulders. "So, we need to make sure there's nothing here that exculpates Rose before Shelia gets her hands on it. In case you didn't notice, Shelia wouldn't exactly be heartbroken if Rose was bound over for trial."

"If there is anything exculpatory here, Harris is obligated to turn it over to me."

"Assuming the police turned it over to him."

"So now Rose is being framed as some part of a huge conspiracy between the Charleston police, Harris and Shelia? Quick, call Oliver Stone. I'm sure there's a movie in here somewhere."

"I like the way your eyes turn dark blue when you're mad."

Joanna shrugged away from him. "Don't try to change the subject. You're welcome to rummage around, but I don't want any part of it."

"Suit yourself."

GABE FOUND nothing in the kitchen, not even when he performed the very unpleasant task of going through the garbage pail. The living room yielded a big zero, as well. Unless he counted the few minutes he was in the same room with Joanna. What was wrong with him? He was like some teenager caught in the first rush of testosterone. The truth was, Joanna fascinated him. She was strength and vulnerability, caution and risk, all wrapped up in a pleasing package. He wondered if she knew just how hard it had been to let her go last night. Or if she guessed that he wouldn't be so gallant given a second chance.

"Are you finished yet?"

He turned to find her standing in the doorway, her eyes still dark with open hostility. "Something is missing."

"Permission to be here?" she suggested snidely.

He let that pass. "Help me out here. I know something isn't right, but I can't put my finger on it."

"We're breaking the law?"

"Dammit, Joanna! I'm serious."

Whether it was his outburst or her fervent desire to leave, he would never know. It didn't much matter, because the end result was just what he needed. Joanna entered the bedroom and began looking around.

"Apparently Joe Don was a tidy guy," she said.

"Probably used one of those organizers."

"Do you want my help or do you want to criticize me?"

"Sorry," Gabe muttered as he got down on his knees and looked under the bed. Nothing.

"The police report said nothing was removed from Joe Don's residence, right?" Joanna called from the small bathroom adjacent to the bedroom.

"Yep," he answered as he got up.

"Then where are the dirty clothes?"

Gabe moved up beside her. "What dirty clothes?"

"That's my point," Joanna said. "I looked in the closet and in the dresser drawers. There were only two pairs of underwear in the dresser, but there's no hamper or laundry bag anywhere in this apartment. Surely Joe Don owned more than three pairs of underwear."

Gabe felt his admiration for the woman before him grow in leaps and bounds. "That's what's missing."

"Let's go talk to the landlady."

They found a woman in her late sixties on the front stoop of the building, snapping green beans into a large pot. Gabe offered her his brightest smile. She returned the gesture, only her smile was minus three front teeth.

Gabe introduced himself and Joanna. "We'd like some information, if you don't mind."

The old woman regarded him for a minute before saying, "Nothing in life is free."

Nodding, Gabe took his money clip from his pants pocket and peeled off several twenty-dollar bills. He ignored Joanna's little grunt of disgust. "What can you tell me about your tenant, Mr. Porter?"

"He's dead."

Gabe smiled indulgently at the crotchety woman. "I didn't give you the money to tell me what I already know."

She shrugged and went back to snapping the beans. "He was a strange one."

"How so?" Gabe asked.

"Classy men like him don't usually choose to live in a dump like this. His clothes was too nice and he talked real educatedlike."

"Speaking of his clothes," Gabe began. "Is there a laundry room in this building?"

The old woman snorted. "Not hardly. But that didn't seem to bother Mr. Porter. He did his laundry real regularlike. Kept his place neat, too. I checked a few times when he wasn't home."

"Where did he do his laundry?" Gabe asked.

She looked up at him; then, using a bruised green bean, she pointed south. "At the Coin-Op two blocks down, same as everybody else."

"Thanks."

"Tell me again why we're doing this," Joanna said to him as they walked the two blocks to the laundry.

"Aren't you curious about what we might find?"

"I'm sure we'll find one of two things," she answered with an edge of annoyance in her tone. "Either we'll have the disgusting task of fondling Joe Don's dirty clothes that have been lying around for weeks, or we'll discover that the owner of the shop made a few dollars by selling the clothes to some of the other customers."

Gabe draped his arm around her shoulder. "That's what I like about you, Jo. You always look on the bright side."

The inside of the laundry was steamy and stale. Gabe walked directly to the back, where a heavyset woman was perched in a cage decorated with signs that read No Checks and No Sharing of Equippment. Equipment was spelled wrong.

"Hi," he said as Joanna eyed him warily. "I'm Gabe Langston and this is Joanna Boudreaux. She's an attorney."

"I was wondering when y'all would get around to comin' here. This is about that white man what got hisself killed."

"Exactly," Gabe answered.

"You'll have to pay the storage fee, same as anyone else."

"No problem," Gabe said as he again reached for his money. "How much?"

The woman spent a few minutes with a nubby pencil and a pad of paper. "Forty-two dollars," she said.

Gabe handed her fifty and said, "Keep it for your troubles."

She smiled. "I didn't know cops tipped."

"We're not—"

"Like your average cops," Gabe finished for Joanna. He gripped her shoulder, warning her to play along.

The woman waddled down from the cage and went to a side door. She returned dragging a canvas bag knotted with a drawstring. "Here's his stuff."

After hoisting the heavy bag onto his shoulder, Gabe hurried Joanna from the building.

"Now we can add impersonating a police officer to our growing list of crimes."

"I didn't tell her we were from the police," Gabe reminded her.

"But you didn't correct her when she made that assumption."

"Lighten up, Jo. We got what we wanted and she's got a few extra dollars in her pocket."

"And you wasted a hundred and fifty dollars for the honor of searching Joe Don's drawers."

Gabe let out an expletive when they rounded the corner and he saw his car. Joanna chuckled beside him.

"It isn't funny," he growled.

"It's poetic justice," she said. "I hope whatever is in that laundry bag is worth the money, the risks and your hubcaps and hood ornament."

"Be quiet, Jo," he warned.

"How much does it cost to replace parts on a Mercedes?"

"Jo," he warned again.

Gabe opened the back passenger door and dumped the contents of the bag onto the seat.

"At least it's clean," Joanna noted.

"And coed," Gabe said as he dipped into the pile and pulled out a lacy pink teddy.

"Too big for Rose and the wrong color," Joanna said as she examined the article he held up by flimsy straps. "And too small for the silicon-enhanced Miss Danforth."

"This isn't Rose," he agreed. "Are you sure it wouldn't fit Michelle?"

"Positive," Joanna answered. "That woman is nearly six feet tall. There's no way she could squeeze into this."

"Start going through the pockets," he instructed.

"What am I looking for?"

"Anything," Gabe answered as he pulled a pair of slacks from the pile.

He had gone through three pairs of slacks, two pairs of shorts and five shirts, when his fingers found a crisp, folded and water-faded slip of paper.

Gingerly, he opened the pale-yellow paper. "I think we hit pay dirt."

"What is it?"

"It's hard to make out," he said as he backed out of the car and held the paper up in the bright sunlight. "'Becket's Jewelry,'" he read. "Dated the day before Joe Don died. One seventeen-inch gold electroplate necklace. Joe Don paid cash. Twenty-four ninety-five plus tax."

Chapter Ten

"There it is!" Joanna exclaimed excitedly. "See if there's parking in that alley next to it."

"I'd prefer to park on the street," Gabe told her.

Joanna patted his arm. "No need. They've already stolen the good parts off this baby."

"Don't remind me," he groaned.

They left the unadorned Mercedes in the alley and made their way back to the small store on the corner of a fairly busy downtown street. Becket's window proclaimed the best prices on gold in town.

"If you happen to be partial to overlay," Joanna muttered as Gabe held the door for her.

"I take it you have expensive tastes?" Gabe asked against her ear.

A small shiver ran along her spine, carrying the warmth of his breath to her whole body. "I have better taste than my checking account will permit. But, yes, I happen to like nice jewelry, probably some genetic defect in the X chromosome."

His soft laughter and the feel of his large hand

splayed across the center of her back brought the butterflies to life in the pit of her stomach.

"May I help you?" a young woman Joanna placed in her late teens or early twenties called to them from behind a glass counter.

Gabe pulled the stiff receipt from his pocket and handed it to the girl. "We'd like some information on the gentleman who bought this necklace."

"Why?" she asked.

Joanna stepped forward. "Because he was murdered a few hours after he made the purchase."

The girl blanched. "These are my initials," she said in a voice splintered by nervousness. "But this was weeks ago and I don't really remember the buyer."

"Mr. Porter was about six feet, black hair," Joanna told her. "A few strands of gray at the temples."

"Oh, right," the girl said as she nodded. "He had the necklace wrapped because she was waiting in the car and he wanted it to be a surprise. He bought a card, too."

"There was a woman with him?" Joanna asked, unable to keep the excitement from her voice. "Can you describe the woman?"

The salesclerk shrugged. "I didn't get a very good look at her. She was sitting in the car, so I only saw her from the side."

"Anything you can tell us would be of help," Gabe said.

"All I remember is her hair."

"That's a start," Joanna prompted. "What color was it?"

The girl raised her hands to either side of her head. "It was teased out to here and bleached that sleazy color blond. Oh, and she had on big earrings, either horses or zebras. Some sort of animal."

"WE DON'T KNOW that to be a fact," Gabe argued.

"Sure," Joanna fumed. "I'm certain there are several women who knew Joe Don who also have over-teased blond hair and animal jewelry. C'mon, she described Rose to a tee."

"The only way we'll know for sure is to ask her."

Joanna gaped at him. "I wish I could understand your attitude when it comes to Rose."

"It's called faith," he answered curtly.

"It's called blind faith," Joanna grumbled. "And why do you get so damned defensive whenever we catch her lying?"

"We don't know that she lied. All we have is a vague description from a girl who probably waits on fifty customers a week."

"And I'll be appointed to the Supreme Court."

Joanna and Gabe drove to the Rose Tattoo in tense silence. She didn't know why he was so sure Rose was innocent, but she did know Rose was a liar. Gabe could argue his theory that the salesgirl was mistaken from now until the end of time and nothing would make her believe that it was anyone other than Rose Porter with Joe Don on the day he died.

"Hi," Lucy greeted them as they entered through the front door. Today was obviously a tribute to the fifties. Lucy had on a tight sweater and a poodle skirt. Her brown wig came complete with flip and headband, and she even had jewel-encrusted glasses and fraternity pin to finish the ensemble.

The fact that Elvis was blasting from the jukebox only added validity to Lucy's getup. If Joanna didn't know better, she might actually believe she had stepped back into the innocent days of American life.

"Hi," she returned. "Is Rose upstairs?"

Lucy cracked the wad of chewing gum and said, "Yep. She's up there with J.D. and Wesley."

"Great." Joanna sighed, not relishing the idea of calling the woman on her lies with her two staunchly supportive sons at her side, and Gabe the Gullible Friend to boot.

"Why don't you wait down here?" she said to him.

"Sorry," he answered as his hand gripped her elbow. "You'll just have to tough it out."

"I hate it when my clients lie to me."

"Before you condemn her for lying, why don't you hear what she has to say?"

Joanna felt as if her body were weighted down as she slowly climbed the stairs with Gabe right on her heels. "Because we both know she'll only deny it."

"Maybe."

Frosty was the only word she could think of to describe the greeting she received from the two Porter men. Rose's reaction wasn't much better and Joanna noted that she went out of her way to avoid eye contact. Not a good sign.

"I need to speak to Rose alone," she told the two men.

"No!" Rose called, apparently panicked by the mere thought. "I mean, my sons are welcome to hear anything I have to say. We don't have any secrets."

Joanna rubbed her temples for a minute, trying to dissolve the tension that was threatening to turn into a full-blown headache. "You might not want them to hear some of the things I need to discuss with you," Joanna said as she sat in a chair vacated by Wesley.

"We're all adults here," J.D. said. "Please don't assume that we aren't interested in how you plan on handling this case."

While she found J.D. a tad on the arrogant side, she had no desire to malign his dead father in front of him.

"It isn't about the case," Joanna said as she turned and met the man's guarded eyes. "We've uncovered a few things regarding your father that aren't exactly flattering."

"Michelle?" J.D. asked.

Joanna looked at Rose, who was sitting with her jaw hanging open.

"Who the hell is Michelle?" Then there was a flash of recognition in her eyes. She looked at Joanna and asked, "Are you talking about Michelle Danforth?"

"Mother," Wesley said as he moved around and

placed a comforting arm around her. "I know you had high hopes for a reconciliation. I honestly believe that's what Dad wanted, as well. He just couldn't seem to remain faithful. Not to you, not to Shelia and probably not to any woman. It was a flaw in his character, not anything you did or didn't do."

Rose's shock melded into a kind of controlled fury that shocked and worried Joanna. She turned to see Gabe standing as far away from the group as possible, like some outsider looking in.

"Are you saying you didn't know about Michelle?"

"Of course she didn't," J.D. growled. "Don't be stupid."

"Watch your attitude, Porter," Gabe warned. "Joanna is only doing her job."

For an instant Joanna wondered if the two men might come to blows. J.D. certainly looked willing and Gabe's hands coiled and uncoiled into fists.

"Stop this," Rose insisted. "J.D., I think you owe Joanna an apology."

"So do I," Gabe said in a voice that communicated a definite threat.

"Actually," Wesley piped up in an artificially cheerful tone, "I happen to agree, big brother. Now, tell the lady you're sorry."

"I'm sorry," J.D. managed, though much like his first apology, it came out sounding as if the words left a foul taste in his mouth.

Stuffing a lock of hair up into the comb keeping it

off her neck, Joanna rubbed her eyes and said, "Okay, I think we all need to back up and start from the beginning."

"The beginning of what?" Rose asked.

"Back to when Joe Don first arrived here in Charleston."

"Gee, that sounds oddly familiar," Gabe said with a sigh as he came over and leaned against the arm of Joanna's chair. "Seems to me I've heard that suggestion before, but I just can't remember whose brilliant idea it was."

"Shut up, Langston," Joanna whispered. "You're a brilliant investigator and I should have listened to you before when you told me to do this. I'm sorry for doubting you, O Great One."

She could see Wesley, J.D. and Rose struggling to keep from laughing and that knowledge caused her face to grow warm from embarrassment.

"I see you two are working well together," Rose said.

She seemed amazingly pleased by the thought, so much so that it apparently was of more importance to her than discovering her former husband was a philanderer.

"I can't think of anyone else I would enjoy working with more," Gabe said on an expelled breath.

"I can," Joanna mumbled.

"She does that because she doesn't want me to know how interested she is."

Joanna was completely humiliated.

"Tory was like that," J.D. volunteered. "Take my advice, Langston. Ignore the barbs and knock down all her perceived obstacles one by one."

"Why, thanks, J.D. I might just give that a try."

"And I might just remove your spleen with an oyster fork."

The three men laughed, as did Rose.

"I'm sorry Dylan isn't here to hear this," Rose said. "I think it would bring back his fond memories of when Shelby was doing her darnedest to pretend she wasn't interested."

"I think we should get back to the subject at hand," Joanna insisted.

"Right," Rose said, sobering instantly. "So, Susan was right? Joe Don was two-timing me?"

"Pretty much," Joanna answered. "I'm sorry Rose, but the DA will surely use this to show motive on your part."

"But I didn't know!"

Joanna turned and looked at J.D. and Wesley in turn. "But the two of you did, right?"

Both men appeared guilty even before they nodded.

"Why didn't you tell me?" Rose demanded. "I can't believe you let me carry on about how well things were going when you knew he was cheating."

"He was our father," J.D. said quietly. "We both told him to be honest with you."

"How long ago did your father tell you he was seeing Michelle Danforth?" Joanna asked.

"Five, maybe six months ago," J.D. answered.

"I only found out three months ago," Wesley admitted. "She answered the phone when I called his house."

"Michelle certainly does have a distinctive voice," Joanna agreed.

"I know," Wesley said. "Her accent is pretty thick."

"Accent?" Joanna, Gabe and J.D. said in unison.

"Very French," Wesley answered.

Joanna looked at Gabe. "Maybe this Frenchwoman is the registered owner of the teddy."

"What teddy?" Rose asked.

Joanna and Gabe took turns telling them what they had found at Joe Don's home and at the laundry. When they were finished, Joanna felt sorry for Rose, but she knew she still had to confront her on several inconsistencies.

"Did Joe Don ever ask you to wear something exotic?"

"Exotic?"

"Michelle Danforth claims that she overheard Joe Don arranging a meeting with a woman and he asked her to dress exotically for the meeting."

"It wasn't me," Rose insisted. "It must have been his little French tart. God." Rose slammed her fist against her desk. "I'm half tempted to go to the cemetery and dig him up just so I can slap his face."

"We found this," Joanna said, ignoring this somewhat ghoulish suggestion, as she passed the receipt for the necklace to Rose. "The salesclerk said that when she sold the necklace to Joe Don, a woman was with him."

"The French tart?" Rose asked.

"Actually..." Joanna hesitated as her eyes fixed on the zebra earrings dangling from Rose's ears. "The description she gave matched you perfectly."

Chapter Eleven

"It wasn't me," Rose insisted. "Ask Shelby. I was here working right up to the time Joe Don met me for dinner."

"How can you be so sure?" Joanna asked. "It was several weeks ago."

"Joe Don was killed on a Monday night. On Mondays I have to inventory and restock the kitchen and the pantry. I didn't leave this building from about eight in the morning until midnight."

Joanna remained skeptical, but she moved on. "Okay, what time did you open that day?"

"Eleven-thirty," Rose answered. "Like always."

"Were you here alone from eight until opening?"

"Shelby came in about nine. Then the chef and the rest of the kitchen staff get here about ten. Susan and Lucy got here about eleven to do setup."

"Did anyone come in that day who didn't belong? Someone who might have had an opportunity to take the gun?"

Rose shook her head. "I let the chef in myself.

Then the back door stays unlocked. No one could get in without going past the crew, and they didn't say anything to me. Why?''

"Because I have to explain away the fact that Joe Don was killed here, with a gun that was secured behind the bar. Think, Rose. Is there any possible way someone could have gotten hold of a spare key?''

"There aren't any spares.''

"Maybe someone accidentally left the front door unlocked.''

Rose shook her head. "I already asked Susan and she swears the front door was locked when she and Lucy came on.''

"Would Susan lend her key to anyone?''

Rose vehemently shook her head. "She won't even let Lucy use it on the days Lucy works and Susan doesn't.''

"Was there ever a time around the murder that your keys disappeared for a little while?''

Rose shook her head and her demeanor could only be described as grim.

"Then let's work this from the other end,'' Gabe said. "Shelia told us that she and Joe Don were happily married and that this Charleston thing was just an opportunity for him to have a change of pace.''

"Hardly,'' Rose snorted.

"Maybe in her dreams,'' J.D. added.

"How long had their marriage been in trouble?'' Joanna asked.

"At least two years," Wesley answered. "Shelia knew he had a girlfriend back in Miami."

"Was she French?" Joanna asked.

"Hispanic," J.D. answered. "But it ended about a year ago when that woman found a man who was willing to leave his wife for her."

"Why Charleston?" Joanna asked.

"He needed money," Rose answered. "At least, that's what he told me."

"Needed money for what?"

"Venture capital," Wesley stated. "He treated the women in his life badly, but he wouldn't dream of taking money from either of his sons."

"I thought he had a thriving business in Miami," Gabe remarked.

Wesley and J.D. shrugged, then Wesley spoke. "I've been in L.A. with Destiny. He only told me that he was returning to Charleston because he was tired of working in Miami and he wanted to get away from Shelia."

"Michelle Danforth impressed me as a lady with no cash-flow problems," Gabe said. "Maybe Joe Don was hoping to seduce her into fronting him the cash to start a new business."

"Did she really impress you as the kind of woman who could be duped by a few whispered endearments?" Joanna asked. "Or were you so taken by the way she crawled all over you that you didn't notice?"

Gabe grinned. "It was one of my more difficult interrogations."

Joanna groaned. "If Joe Don had a successful business in Florida, why didn't he just use that for collateral for a loan?"

"When I spoke to him the week before he died, Dad said he had found a partner and he expected to begin operations within a month."

Wesley absently toed the edge of the carpet with his shoe. "Dad told me something else."

"What?" Joanna asked.

"He said that this partnership would solve his Florida problems."

"What Florida problems?" Gabe asked.

Wesley shook his head. "I don't know, but I think it had something to do with money."

Gabe locked his eyes on her. Joanna swallowed, knowing full well that Wesley had just provided what might be an important bit of information.

Gabe rubbed his hand over his neatly tied-back hair. "If your father was having financial troubles in Florida, what's Shelia doing in a suite at the Omni?"

"Our stepmother has a certain comfort level," J.D. explained. "Shelia likes nice things."

"And other women's husbands," Rose grumbled.

Joanna's mind was racing in several directions. If there was a problem in Florida, she could use it in court. But only if she could somehow connect Joe Don's life nine months ago in another state to his death in Charleston. Then there was her gut feeling that Rose was still holding something back. If she was the partner...

"Rose," Joanna pleaded. "Tell me you weren't going to lend Joe Don any money."

Rose chuckled. "I don't have it to lend. Shelby and I are just now beginning to turn a real profit. I had to borrow up to my eyeballs to keep my half of this place. I'm still paying off those debts."

"Who do you owe?" Joanna asked.

"I've paid off everyone but a few hundred dollars to Mitch Fallon."

"Mitch Fallon?" Joanna repeated. "He's on the prosecution's witness list."

"I can't imagine why. The only connection we have is the loan," Rose claimed.

"So who was Joe Don getting this money from?"

"Peter Danforth," Gabe replied.

"It's a possibility," Joanna hedged. "I guess for now he should top the list."

"Then I suggest we pay him a visit."

"Wait," Rose said as Joanna and Gabe stood. "Do you know anything about Peter Danforth?"

"He's Michelle's brother. Makes the financial pages every now and again," Gabe answered. "He's old money and he's got a pretty good reputation for making more."

Joanna walked to the doorway and stopped. "Rose, can you think of any reason your landlady is on the witness list?"

Rose's facade faltered slightly, but she said no in a clear, steady voice.

"I still think she's hiding something," Joanna told

Gabe as they walked through the kitchen and entered the now-busy dining area.

"I think you only do that so you don't have to deal with the pressure of knowing your client is innocent."

"Right," Joanna breathed. "And you're in for a big letdown when we lose at the prelim."

"Hey," Gabe began as he caught her arm. "You aren't giving up, are you?"

She looked up into his eyes. "I'm not giving up, Gabe. I'm just a little more realistic than you are. And please let go of me. People are staring."

"You all right?" a dark-haired man asked as he came to Joanna's side.

She was about to answer, when she saw the huge grin on the man's face when he looked at Gabe.

"Sorry, Gabe. I didn't realize—"

"Forget it," Gabe said as he gave the man's hand a masculine shake. "Dylan Tanner, this is Joanna Boudreaux."

"Rose's attorney," Dylan surmised. "Shelby is beside herself with worry. Rose was a rock when Chad was kidnapped. I don't think Shelby could have made it through that without her support. If there's anything we can do…"

"Actually," Joanna said, her thoughts racing, "you're DEA, right?"

"Yes."

"Is there any way you can get me a list of female French nationals or French Canadians who arrived in Charleston in the past six months?"

"Sure," Dylan responded without hesitation. "When do you need it?"

"Yesterday," she said with a smile.

"Then I'd better get going. Nice to meet you."

"Same here," Joanna told him.

"Why so quiet?" Gabe asked when they reached the car.

"I was just thinking about what Dylan said."

"About Chad?"

Joanna nodded. "I can't imagine how awful it must be to go through something like that."

She noticed he was frowning when he slid behind the wheel. "What?"

Gabe started the engine. "Is that why you don't have any children?"

Joanna let out a small laugh. "Update, Gabe. I'm not married and—"

"A lot of women like you don't wait for Mr. Right to come along to procreate."

"Women like me?"

"Career women, and before you get yourself into a feminist knot, I'm not using that term as an epithet. I'm amazed it took as long as it did for women to feel comfortable with balancing a family and a career."

"How egalitarian of you," Joanna retorted. "But just for the record, women would have been comfortable with it for centuries. Men and ridiculous laws kept them from realizing their goals."

"I surrender," Gabe said. "You can stop staring daggers at me."

"Sorry, I guess I'm a little oversensitive when it comes to this issue. Before my father died he told me he had only one regret."

"That he hadn't walked you down the aisle?" Gabe guessed.

"No. That he would never see any of his grandchildren."

"But I'll bet he was proud of you."

Joanna's melancholy ended immediately. "Very."

"My father found me a continual source of embarrassment. I think it drove him nuts that in spite of his guiding and prodding, I never did develop his passion for business."

"But I'll bet he was proud of you."

Gabe shrugged. "I have no idea. We didn't speak to each other after my twentieth birthday."

"That's sad," Joanna said. "But that does explain where you get your stubborn streak."

"I was adopted," he reminded her.

"Nurture versus nature," Joanna said as she reached across the console and placed her hand on his leg. "I don't know how we got on this morose subject."

"There's nothing morose about the way you're touching my leg," Gabe told her as he made a sudden and illegal U-turn.

"What are you doing?"

"A slight change in plans," he said.

"But what about Danforth and the ton of work I have to do?"

"You'll get it all done—just not this instant."

"Gabe," Joanna breathed as she grew more annoyed. "What do you think you're doing?"

"What I should have done about a week ago."

"What the hell is that supposed to mean?" Joanna demanded as she pulled her hand away from him as if he were some sort of disgusting creature.

"It means that we're changing the focus of our investigation."

"We are not."

"Yes," he said tightly, "we are. I've indulged you, now you'll have to indulge me."

"This isn't about indulging. I have to prepare for the hearing. I need to interview the people on Harris's list. I need to formulate a strategy. I need to spend time with Rose in case I decide to present a defense at the hearing. I need—"

"To lighten up and trust me," Gabe cut in. "We'll make a quick trip to Miami."

"Joe Don wasn't killed in Miami."

Gabe was forced to stop for a traffic light. He turned and looked at her, his expression conveying his enthusiasm. "Joe Don was killed because of money," he insisted.

"You can prove that?"

She watched as impatience dampened his enthusiasm. "You have to trust me, Jo. I know what I'm doing and I know I'm right."

"Just as you know Rose is innocent?"

Gabe frowned. "We're going to Miami."

"You're welcome to go to Miami," she countered. "Just drop me off at my office and then you're welcome to chase your tail through all fifty states."

"You're coming with me."

"Wrong."

"I CAN'T BELIEVE I let you talk me into this," she stormed as she buckled her seat belt. "I have a ton of work I should be doing."

"You're working," Gabe assured her. "And we'll only stay one night."

He watched as she slammed her head back against the soft leather seat in the first-class cabin of the commercial airliner. His gut told him that this was the right way to go. Joanna would realize that as soon as they had a true picture of Joe Don's life prior to the murder.

"Even if you find something in Miami," Joanna argued, "it won't explain how someone got into the locked Rose Tattoo and used a gun that was kept behind the bar."

He rubbed his temples. "When we know the who, we'll be able to figure out the how and the why."

"I hate to disillusion you," Joanna said on a breath, "but Rose looks pretty good as the who."

"She's not a killer."

"You're that sure?"

"Absolutely."

"How do you know that?"

Gabe reached out and tapped her nose with his forefinger. "You'll just have to trust me on this."

She swatted his hand away. "Like I have a choice. I can't believe you talked me into getting on a plane without letting me pack a bag."

He smiled at her. "Live dangerously, Jo. Shop at the hotel store."

"Right. The markup in those places is about a trillion percent."

"I'm paying."

"No, you aren't," she said firmly. "I may not be in your socioeconomic bracket, but I can afford my own hotel room."

Gabe merely smiled. Apparently she didn't care much for the gesture, since she made a small, frustrated sound before offering him her back and silently staring out the window for the remainder of the short flight.

"This is a colossal waste of time," Joanna huffed as they walked up the gangway from the aircraft.

"Not if we find the killer."

"Will he be waiting for us in the airport?" she asked sweetly. "Maybe he'll be holding up a sign that says Welcome to Miami. I'm Your Killer."

"Cute, Jo." He took a deep breath. "Follow me."

"That's what I've been doing and it's costing me precious time."

"Stop whining, Jo."

"I don't whine."

"Then stop nagging."

"I don't nag."

"Then stop talking."

He led her to the rental-car-agency counter, where he rented a car. Gabe stopped at the bank of courtesy telephones near the exit. While he waited for the hotel to take his reservation he studied Joanna.

She looked positively furious, and incredibly desirable. He blinked once, trying to keep his mind from wandering into the recurring fantasy of peeling off her shirt and shorts. He would start by removing her sandals to massage each dainty foot in turn. He could almost feel the silky smoothness of her shapely legs as his eyes moved where his hands could not. Then he would carry her to the bed and—"

"You're confirmed for this evening."

A female voice interrupted his fantasy.

"Sir?"

"Fine," Gabe said, raising his voice because of the construction going on just outside the exit door. "We should be arriving in about thirty minutes. Have a bottle of champagne and a cheese-and-fruit tray waiting."

"Yes, Mr. Langston. Anything else?"

"We'll be needing some things from the store."

"I'll alert the staff."

"Thank you."

After breaking the connection, Gabe took Joanna's elbow and led her from the building. As they walked along the sidewalk, they were forced to dodge a number of bright-orange cones and chipped hunks of concrete. The sound of a jackhammer was nearly deafening as it echoed through the concrete parking garage adjacent to the walkway.

As he was following the signs that directed him to the rental lot, Gabe felt something hit his head. Thinking it might be an unwelcome gift from a bird flying overhead, he stopped and raised his hand to cautiously touch the spot.

His fingers came away with a powdery substance he immediately recognized as cement. It was then that he glanced up. As if seeing it in slow motion, Gabe watched as a huge hunk of the concrete ledge broke free of the building right above their heads.

Chapter Twelve

Joanna felt the air rush from her body as something heavy and hard crushed her. She was showered with tiny pebblelike shards that stung her hands. It seemed like forever before the heavy weight was lifted off her.

"Are you all right?" Gabe asked as he pulled her to her feet.

She leaned forward, sucking in deep breaths as tears stung her eyes. Her chest burned, but she managed to nod.

"Are you folks hurt?"

Gabe ignored the security guard, his whole attention on Joanna.

"We're fine," she told him in a raspy voice. Then, looking at Gabe, her demeanor changed immediately. "You're bleeding," she said as she straightened, got up on her tiptoes and brushed his hair away from the wound on his forehead.

"So are you." Gabe took her hand and turned gently to inspect a long abrasion on her forearm.

"I'll call an ambulance," the guard offered.

"That isn't necessary," Gabe said. "These are just scrapes. We'll take care of it back at our hotel."

When Joanna looked at Gabe, she sensed something was wrong. When she opened her mouth to speak, he silenced her with a subtle shake of his head.

"I'll take you folks up to the office," the guard said.

"That won't be necessary," Gabe said.

The wiry man appeared upset. "But I need to fill out a report for our insurance company."

"We aren't going to sue," Gabe informed the man.

"But—"

"I'm a lawyer," Joanna told the man in an attempt to assuage his fears. "Neither one of us is hurt, so there isn't any problem."

"But—"

Gabe reached down near the pile of concrete rubble and retrieved the key to their rental car. A small crowd had gathered, but they parted when Gabe took her hand and led her off.

"I guess we know why they had parts of the walkway cordoned off," Joanna mused as she began to inventory the assortment of scrapes and cuts on her arms.

"Something like that," Gabe answered ominously.

"What is that supposed to mean?"

"Don't you think it's a little too coincidental that a huge hunk of concrete almost kills us just a few minutes after we arrive?"

Joanna considered his paranoid comment. "It couldn't be anything but a coincidence," she told him as they reached the car parked in the spot that corresponded to the number on the key chain. "No one knows we're here except for Rose and my secretary."

Joanna looked at him across the top of the car. "Your theory would mean that Rose arranged to have us killed."

"Don't be silly," Gabe snapped. "What about your secretary? Is she trustworthy?"

Joanna laughed. "Tammy works part-time so she can be home with her four kids in the afternoons. She's about as likely to contract a murder as I am."

Gabe yanked the car door open. "Well, something about this just doesn't feel right."

"Accidents happen," Joanna said as she slipped into the seat. "I didn't know you could rent these."

"I happen to be partial to Mercedes. They're well-built machines."

Joanna just nodded. The car wasn't the only well-built thing. Nope. All she had to do was close her eyes and she could remember the feel of his large body on hers. "Why did you do it?"

"Do what?"

"Throw yourself on top of me?"

"It seemed like a good idea at the time."

"Go ahead and make a joke out of it." Joanna sighed. "We could have been killed if you hadn't reacted so quickly."

He turned and gave her a brilliant smile and a playful little wink. "Are you grateful?"

"Of course." She was suddenly uncomfortable, though she couldn't quite decide why.

"You know, in some cultures you'd be forced to repay me by pledging your life to me in return."

"Nice try, Sultan Langston, but I'm not pledging anything."

Gabe chuckled. "It was worth a shot."

The doorman at the elegant hotel eyed them suspiciously until Gabe handed him a generous tip along with the keys to the rental. It was only when they approached the entrance that Joanna fully understood the man's hesitation. "Why didn't you tell me I looked like some refugee?" Joanna wailed as she began a futile attempt to brush the dust and cement from her hair.

"It'll all wash off," he promised.

"But my clothes are ruined."

"Clothes are replaceable."

"You have all the answers, don't you?" Joanna grumbled as they entered the gilded foyer of the expensive hotel. "If we're only staying one night, why did you have to pick the most expensive place in town?"

Gabe made a disgusted noise. "I thought we agreed that you would stop talking."

"I'm not wasting hundreds of dollars on a bed and a shower," she argued. She stopped and grabbed his shirtsleeve. "Let's go someplace else."

"I like it here," he replied as he shrugged off her hand. "I'm also bleeding, hungry and dirty, so stop acting like we're about to check into the Bates Motel."

"But, Gabe?" she pressed.

He glared down at her. "I just saved your life, Jo. I think that entitles me to just a small amount of latitude from you."

She snapped her mouth closed and remained silent as he registered. She was also silent when he dragged her into the pricey shop near the elevators and ordered her to pick out clothing.

"Three hundred dollars for a bathrobe?" Joanna fairly shrieked. "That's obscene."

"The price is reflective of the quality of the item," a snooty woman with bluish hair and a pointy nose directed toward the ceiling informed her.

"The price is reflective of a generous markup," Joanna countered.

"She'll take it," Gabe said as he yanked the robe from the display rack. Then, reading the size, he selected a dress and instructed the saleswoman to include appropriate undergarments and have them sent to their room.

The routine was repeated in the swanky men's shop before Joanna and Gabe got on the elevator. He put a special key in a slot on the control panel and the elevator began its ascent.

"You're very adept at wasting money," Joanna groused.

"It's my money," he answered easily. "Don't worry about it."

"Fine," she agreed. "But I insist on paying for my room."

Gabe chuckled. Joanna was about to ask what he found so humorous, when the doors to the elevator opened, revealing a huge suite.

"What the hell is this?" she asked. "You rented the presidential suite for one night?"

"It's not the presidential," Gabe told her as he sauntered into the spacious living room and tossed the key on a coffee table. "It's the royal suite."

"Excuse me," Joanna snapped as she began to explore the place. She discovered that in addition to a large living room, there was a huge bathroom, complete with soaking tub, and a giant bedroom with a bed the size of a football field. Everything was decorated in a Grecian motif, right down to the platter of fruit and bottle of champagne in the living room.

"There's only one bedroom," Joanna announced when she stood before him.

Gabe was on the sofa, popping grapes into his mouth. There were two glasses of champagne on the table. "I know."

"I thought we came here to investigate."

"We did."

Joanna was getting angrier by the second. "Then what's with the champagne and the fruit and the giant-size bed beneath the mirror on the ceiling?"

Gabe's expression brightened. "There's a mirror?"

"Langston…" Joanna warned.

She was cut off when the elevator opened and a porter came in carrying an assortment of hangers and boxes. Gabe directed him into the bedroom, then peeled off several bills once the young man had done his job.

"You can have the shower first," he said as soon as they were alone.

"I'm not staying here," Joanna announced.

He shrugged, downed the glass of champagne in one long swallow and hoisted himself off the couch. "Suit yourself. I'm going to get cleaned up."

"Suit yourself," she mimicked when he'd left the room. At the sink of the bar, Joanna managed to make herself presentable. Or as presentable as she could get with a layer of dust and dirt decorating her formerly white shorts.

After scribbling a curt note telling Langston she would call and let him know where he could retrieve the rental car, she grabbed the car keys and her now-scuffed leather purse and left the suite.

When the elevator dropped her in the lobby, she accidentally barreled into an impeccably dressed gentleman. "Sorry," she mumbled as she hurried toward to the concierge's desk.

The concierge eyed her as if she were some sort of invading disease. He did everything but hold a handkerchief over his mouth to answer her questions.

"Thanks," she said tightly as she took the map from him. "How do I get to the garage?"

"You have a vehicle?" he asked, clearly surprised.

"I flew in on a broom," she told him. "It's in the valet lot."

"You can simply have the attendant—"

"I'm in a bit of a hurry," Joanna interrupted.

"Take the elevator down to the garage. Valet is located in the far east portion."

"Far east portion," she repeated as she went back to the elevator. "What am I, Marco Polo?"

The elevator was pretty full, but she managed to squeeze on. There was an advantage to being short, she decided. She was the first one off, so she made a guess and turned to the right. The underground lot was dark, cool and really big. Instantly she regretted her impatience with the concierge. It would take her forever to find Gabe's car.

She scanned row after row, walking downhill as the grade of the floor sloped. It was a few seconds before she realized that she could no longer hear the voices of the other hotel guests. In fact, she could only hear one thing—the echo of her footsteps. It was another second before she realized it wasn't an echo, but the sound of someone else.

When she stopped, she could still hear the even, purposeful footfalls, but a quick survey of the shadowy garage revealed nothing.

Joanna took a calming breath and told herself she was being silly. She cursed Gabe. It was probably his ramblings about the accident at the airport not being an accident that had her so edgy. Well, she wasn't about to let his paranoia make her strange. She listened for another second, and hearing nothing, she turned back around and found herself face-to-face with the man she had bumped into at the elevators. Only now he had a rather large, very sharp knife in his hand.

Chapter Thirteen

"Don't make a sound, Joanna," he said. "We're going to take a little walk together."

"Whatever you say," she agreed, remembering all those self-defense classes. "The knife isn't necessary."

He smiled, or rather sneered, revealing a gold front tooth with a diamond chip embedded right in the center. "Let's go."

Joanna's brain went into overdrive. If a rapist takes you to a separate location, your chances of being killed increased something like one hundred percent.

"Move!" he shouted, waving the knife for effect.

She took a tentative step, refusing to give in to the panic welling up inside her. Her purse wouldn't work as a weapon. He probably wouldn't just stand there while she lifted it overhead and took aim. Joanna focused on the keys in her hand. As quietly as she could, she maneuvered the keys so that the elongated portion protruded from her fist. She kept walking, slightly slowing her pace so that her captor had no choice but to come up almost even with her. He had the advantage of height and reach, but she, God willing, had the element of surprise.

Sucking in a breath, Joanna summoned all her courage and stabbed him just below the rib cage, then dropped to the pavement just in time to save herself from the arc of his knife.

She rolled beneath a series of parked cars, then scrambled to get to her feet. In the process, she grabbed on to the door handle of one of the cars, and suddenly the concrete cavern filled with the blaring of a car alarm.

He was holding his side, and if ever she had seen murder in a person's eyes, it was at that instant. A single car separated them. Joanna dropped the keys and started down the row, yanking on every car as she went.

It wasn't long before the man decided to cut his losses. But not before he raised his hand, pointed a gun at her, then pulled the trigger.

"I AM NOT an auto thief. I'm an attorney," Joanna fumed as she was unceremoniously dumped into a chair at the desk of a Detective Michael Simms. "Can we take these handcuffs off, please?"

The plump, balding man in the rumpled short-sleeved shirt gave her a bored look.

"Open my wallet and you'll find my business card."

He didn't budge. Instead he pulled a form from one

of his desk drawers and loaded it into a dated typewriter.

"Name?"

Joanna clamped her lips closed. This finally seemed to get the attention of the detective. The wheels squeaked as he shifted and turned to her. "Hotel security says they caught you trying to steal a car from their garage."

Joanna shook her head. "I tried to tell them what was happening, but they didn't believe me."

The detective picked up the sheet of paper that the patrol officers had left when they turned her over to him. "The concierge said you were acting strangely and that you insisted on being told where the valet cars were parked."

"I was in a hurry and I was only borrowing a car—"

The detective nodded and started to turn back to the typewriter.

"Wait!" she yelled. "I didn't mean it like that. I was borrowing a car that belonged to the man I was staying at the hotel with."

It was immediately apparent that the detective had misconstrued her meaning. "I'm not a hooker, either."

"Whatever," the detective said with a sigh. "Name?"

Joanna opened and closed her hands to keep her fingers from going numb because of the handcuffs.

She was feeling the sting of frustrated tears, when a loud voice drew her attention.

Along with everyone else in the squad room, Joanna craned her neck to find the source. Gabe, his dark hair still damp, was marching through the room, his hazel eyes ablaze.

"Are you all right?" he asked Joanna.

"I will be if you can convince this guy that I'm not a car thief or a hooker."

Gabe's harsh features relaxed as a smile slowly replaced the determined frown. "A hooker?"

"Who are you?" the detective asked, at the same time flipping the snap on his shoulder holster.

"Gabriel Langston," Gabe answered without looking at the man. "Miss Boudreaux is a friend of mine."

"Great," the detective said without inflection. "You can wait for her out there. It'll be a couple of hours."

"Hours?" Joanna parroted. "Do something," she pleaded.

Gabe reached for the detective's telephone. "How do I get an outside line?"

The man appeared annoyed by Gabe's arrogance. "You go out into the waiting area and use a pay phone."

Gabe then glared at the man and said, "Miss Boudreaux is an attorney. If you don't mind a huge lawsuit for false imprisonment..."

"Dial nine, then the number."

Gabe did so, referring to a matchbook as he dialed. He said a few words into the receiver, then handed it to Simms.

The detective's face changed dramatically before he sheepishly put the phone back. "It would seem there has been a misunderstanding," he said as he came around and unlocked the cuffs.

Joanna rubbed her sore wrists and she looked up to see Gabe positively furious as he noticed the dark red bands left by the metal restraints. "There was a misunderstanding, all right," she said. "I was attacked in the garage."

Gabe knelt in front of her and took her hands in his. "Were you hurt?"

Joanna offered him a weak smile. The concern in his voice and in his eyes made her heart flutter and pulse erratic. "Nope. I did the car-key-in-the-fist thing and then ran around triggering car alarms until he ran."

Gabe reached up and stroked her chin. "Did he...?" He didn't finish the thought.

"No, he just scared me."

"My sincere apologies," Detective Simms said as he removed the form from his typewriter and replaced it with another one. "I'll need a description."

Joanna described the man for the detective, while Gabe stood at her side, massaging her shoulder. She drew strength from his touch and managed to get through the ordeal in just under an hour.

Satisfied that she had given the police detective everything, she started to stand, when the memory flashed back. Her knees buckled and she plopped back into the seat. Gabe took his fingertips and raised her chin so that their eyes met.

"What is it?"

"He called me by name."

"What?"

"He called me 'Joanna,'" she repeated.

"So there's a possibility that you were acquainted with your attacker?" Detective Simms asked. "Maybe you defended him or prosecuted him and he wasn't thrilled with the outcome."

Joanna shook her head. "I'd have remembered him. That tooth is very pronounced."

"Come on," Gabe said as he wrapped one arm around her shoulders and helped her to her feet. "I'll take you back to the hotel and—"

"It's better if she looks through the mug books while the face is still fresh in her mind," Simms protested.

"Absolutely not," Gabe stated. "I'll bring her back in the morning. That should give you enough time to pull any photos that even remotely resemble this guy."

Simms looked as if he might argue, but Gabe's tone of voice was enough to keep the man quiet. With a resigned nod, he said goodbye to Joanna and repeated his apology one last time.

"It's dark," she said as they exited the police station and got into a waiting cab. "Why didn't you drive?"

Gabe smiled at her before pulling her into the circle of his arms. Her head rested against his chest and she drank in his scent, while the even rhythm of his breathing calmed her frazzled nerves.

"Someone we both know took the keys."

"Sorry," Joanna murmured as she flattened her palm above his heart. "They're in the garage."

"The rental agency is sending over a spare set. Besides, the car keys aren't important." He punctuated the remark by placing a gentle kiss on the top of her head.

"How can you stand to do that?" Joanna asked. "I must smell like a combination of construction dust and engine exhaust. I'm covered in oil smears and grime."

"But you're safe."

"Good point. Maybe Simms is right. Maybe he was someone I prosecuted."

"You have to promise me something," Gabe said in an urgent tone.

"What?"

"You don't go anywhere without me. I can't believe I was stupid enough to leave the keys lying around. I should have been more careful."

Joanna looked up and met his eyes. "You can't seriously believe that there was anything you could have done to prevent what happened in the garage."

"I should have insisted that you stay in the room."

Joanna let out a small laugh. "You aren't my keeper, Langston. I was so furious when I left that room that there was nothing you could have said or done that would have stopped me."

"I'm bigger than you are."

"Yes," she said as she placed her cheek against his chest again. "You are that."

As soon as they returned to their suite, Joanna gladly shed her clothes and slipped into the deep soaking tub filled with bubbles and soothing warm water. The air was heavy with the scent of lilac as she scooted lower, twisting her already washed hair into a knot on top of her head as the water tickled her chin. She let out a soft moan as her poor body relaxed and the water worked its magic.

"Knock, knock," Gabe said as he entered the room, balancing two glasses of champagne and the bottle in one hand.

"I'm not dressed," Joanna yelped as she arranged the bubbles discreetly over herself. "Go away."

As if he hadn't heard her protest, Gabe came to the edge of the tub and arranged the bottle and the glasses. "Here," he said as he held out a glass. "You can probably use this."

"I could use some privacy."

Gabe was undeterred. His eyes roamed over her face, silently studying her features. "Are you really doing okay?"

Accepting the glass in his hand, she took a sip before answering, "Mostly."

"Want to talk about it?"

"Not especially," she told him. "I'd like to forget it ever happened."

Gabe smiled. "I guessed that would be your reaction." He put his glass down, then took hers, then went and got one of the huge bath towels. "I know just the thing to make you forget."

Joanna eyed him suspiciously.

He smiled. "I see you need some persuasion."

Leaving the towel at the tub's edge, he placed one hand on either side of her head and kissed her slowly and thoroughly. Joanna felt her skin warm as his tongue sparred with hers. It was some time before Gabe lifted his head. When he did, his eyes glowed with unspent desire.

"Either you get out, or I get in. Which will it be?"

"I'll get out," she said. "But not with you standing there watching."

He gave a disappointed nod of agreement. "You have three minutes, then I'm coming back."

The instant he had taken the champagne and left the room, Joanna jumped out of the tub and dried herself. Her fingers were trembling as she belted the obscenely priced robe at her waist. She managed to get a comb through her curly hair, but she knew her time was running out.

She looked at her reflection and asked, "Do you want to do this?" Her finger went to her lip and she remembered his kiss. That memory brought an instant flush to her cheeks. "Of course you do," she whispered. "The man is perfect." She vividly recalled how he had looked when he had stormed the police station to rescue her. It was the most chivalrous thing any man had ever done for her. "Then why are you hesitating?" She sighed. "Because there's a big difference between 'I love you' and 'I want you,'" she acknowledged. "He doesn't love me. As soon as Rose is convicted, I'll never see him again." That thought stung her heart. Then, sucking in a fortifying breath, she said, "So I'll just have to enjoy here and now. It will have to be enough." God, she thought as she headed for the door, she sounded like some Victorian bride who was about to do her duty. "Something tells me I won't want to close my eyes and think of England."

"Two minutes and fifty-eight seconds," Gabe said as she joined him in the living room.

She swallowed and wondered why she suddenly felt so nervous and awkward. The fact that he stood before her, gloriously naked to the waist could have something to do with it. The sight of his beautifully bared, muscular torso made her throat dry and her palms moist. Her eyes followed the thick mat of dark hair until it tapered to a thin line and disappeared into the waistband of his jeans.

Gabe took a step toward her and she took an involuntary step backward as he came close. The action didn't go unnoticed, not if his satisfied smile was any indication.

"Gabe," she cautioned as she held one hand palm out. "We aren't going to do this."

"I haven't done anything," he purred.

Joanna backed up farther, only to find herself against the cool wall. Gabe kept coming, his piercing and hungry eyes belying the small smile curving his chiseled mouth.

"Please? I'm not as good at this as you are. I thought I could just waltz out here and—"

Without a word, Gabe flattened his palms against the wall on either side of her head.

She could smell his musky cologne and hear his slightly uneven breath. There was a smoldering intensity in his eyes that sent a ripple of desire into the pit of her stomach.

"I liked the 'please' part," he teased. "Please what?"

His warm, mint-scented breath washed over her face. Tilting her head back, she searched his eyes beneath the thick outline of his inky lashes.

"I've been very, very patient," he said.

Bending at the waist, Gabe leaned forward until his lips barely grazed hers. Wide-eyed, Joanna experienced the first tentative seconds of the kiss through a haze of indecision. The pressure from his mouth increased almost instantly. It was no longer tentative. It was demanding and confident, apparently fueled by the days of accidental touches and meaningful looks that punctuated their relationship.

His hands moved slowly, purposefully, to her

waist. His strong fingers found the hastily tied knot and made quick work of dispatching it. Then his hand slipped beneath the fabric and came to rest just below the swell of her rib cage. Her mouth burned where he incited fires with his expert exploration. A sigh inspired by purely animal desire rose in her throat. She was being bombarded with so many sensations at once, each one more pleasurable than the last. The calloused pad of his thumb brushed the bared flesh at her midriff. His kiss was so thorough, so wonderful, that her knees were actually beginning to tremble.

When he pulled away, Joanna very nearly reached out to keep him close to her. It wasn't necessary—he didn't go far. Resting his forehead on hers, she listened to the harmony of their labored breathing.

"What are we doing?" he rasped.

"I believe you just kissed me."

"I kissed you. You responded. Why have we spent so much time fighting this?"

"I didn't know we were," she said, feeling sad and lonely all of a sudden. "Maybe we both know this isn't such a great idea."

"That," he began as he lifted his head and met her eyes, "is the dumbest thing I've ever heard you say."

Gabe wasn't subtle with his second kiss. There was nothing even remotely sweet about it. This kiss was meant to do one thing—convey desire. Even before he pressed his hardness into her belly, Joanna knew he was aroused in a way he'd never been before. She also knew that she should keep this from happening, no matter how much she wanted it herself.

"Don't," she said as she placed her hands flat against his chest and gave a little shove. "This is wrong."

"How can you say that?" he countered.

She watched him from behind the safety of her lashes. "I don't do this sort of thing. I don't sleep around for the hell of it."

"Joanna." He said her name on a rush of breath. "I don't want to make love to you for the hell of it."

"Then why?" she asked, truly confused.

He looked at her with eyes so full of tenderness she almost sighed.

"I want to make love to you because you're a very desirable, intelligent, beautiful woman. The normal healthy reasons a man wants a woman." He brushed his lips across her forehead. "I want you to forget all the terrible things that happened today," he insisted as his fingers moved to grip her upper arms. His lips touched hers. His voice deepened to a husky whisper as he continued. "We've been working side by side for weeks. Like it or not, this is more than garden-variety lust. Believe me."

He kissed her lightly.

"I love the way you laugh. I love the fire in your eyes when you're angry. I even love the way you've tried to put me in my place."

"Gabe?" she whispered, feeling her defenses crumble.

"Don't fight me, Joanna, please. I know it will be incredible between us and I don't think I can continue pretending that I don't feel what I'm feeling right now. What I think you feel, too."

"But I need more," she said, still unsure.

He kissed her with equal measures of passion and pleading. "I'll give you everything, Joanna. Trust me."

"You're confusing me," she admitted.

"I'm trying not to," he said quietly. His hand came up and he captured a lock of her hair between his thumb and forefinger. He quietly studied the red strands, his expression dark and intense.

"I don't know what to do, Gabe. I don't want to make a mistake."

"You won't," he promised, his voice low, almost seductive.

The sincerity in his words worked like a vise on her throat. The lump of emotion threatened to strangle her as the moments of silence dragged on.

"We don't have anything in common. We want different things."

"We've never talked about what we wanted," he countered, his voice rising a notch. "We can do that, Joanna. Later," he said as he scooped her off the floor, cradling her against his solid chest.

Gabe carried her down the hall to the bedroom. As if she were some fragile object, he placed her on the bed, gently arranging her against the pillows.

Joanna remained silent as she watched him shed

his remaining clothing without even the slightest hint of embarrassment before he joined her on the bed. Through passion-dilated eyes, she took in the impressive sight of him. Rolling on his side, Gabe pulled her closer, until she encountered the solid outline of his body. His expression was fixed, his mouth little more than a taut line.

"I'll make it good, Joanna. You'll see," he said as he tenderly pulled her into the circle of his arms.

It felt so good, so right. She needed this, needed his strength. She surrendered to the promise she felt in his touch.

Cradling her in one arm, Gabe used his free hand to stroke the hair away from her face. She greedily drank in the scent of his cologne as she cautiously allowed her fingers to rest against his thigh. His skin was warm, and smooth, a startling contrast to the very defined muscle she could feel beneath her hand. She remained perfectly still, comforted by his scent, his touch and his nearness. Strange that she could only find such solace in his arms. Being here in this room with Gabe was enough to erase the frustrations that had plagued her for weeks. What could be the harm in just a few hours of the pleasure she knew she could find here?

"Joanna?" he asked on a strained breath. He captured her face in his hands, his thumbs teasing her cheekbones. His pale eyes met and held hers. His jaw was set, his expression serious. "I don't know if I have the strength to let you get up and walk away from me now. Please tell me this is what you want. Please?''

Using his hands, he tilted her head back. His face was mere fractions of an inch from hers. She could feel the ragged expulsion of his breath. Instinctively, her palms flattened against his chest. The thick mat of dark hair served as a cushion for her touch. Still, beneath the softness, she could easily feel the hard outline of muscle.

''I want you so badly,'' he said in a near-whisper.

Her lashes fluttered as his words washed over her upturned face. She needed to hear those words, perhaps even wished for them. Gabe's lips tentatively brushed hers. So featherlight was the kiss that she wasn't even certain it could qualify as such. His movements were careful, measured. His thumbs stroked the hollows of her cheeks.

Joanna banished all thought from her mind. She wanted this, almost desperately. The touch of his hands and his lips made her feel alive. The ache in her chest was changing, evolving into some new emotion. She became acutely aware of every aspect of him. The pressure of his thigh where it touched hers. The sound of his uneven breathing.

When he lifted his head, Joanna grabbed his broad shoulders. ''Don't,'' she whispered, urging him back to her.

His resistance was both surprising and short-lived. It was almost totally forgotten when he dipped his head. His lips did more than brush against hers. His hands left her face and wound around her small body. Gabe crushed her against him. She could actually feel the pounding of his heart beneath her hands.

The encounter quickly turned into something intense and consuming. His tongue moistened her slightly parted lips. The kiss became demanding and she was a very willing participant. She managed to work her hands across his chest, until she felt the outline of his erect nipples beneath her palms. He responded to her action by tearing off her robe and running his hands all over her back and nibbling her lower lip. It was a purely erotic action, one that inspired great need and desire in Joanna.

A small moan escaped her lips as she kneaded the muscles of his chest. He tasted vaguely of mint and he continued to work magic with his mouth. Joanna felt the kiss in the pit of her stomach. What had started as a pleasant warmth had grown into a full-fledged heat emanating from her very core, fueled by the sensation of his fingers snaking up her back, entwining in her hair and guiding her head back at a severe angle. Passion flared as he hungrily devoured first her mouth, then the tender flesh at the base of her throat. His mouth was hot, the stubble of his beard slightly abrasive. And she felt it all. She was aware of everything—the outline of his body, the almost arrogant expectation in his kiss. Gabe was obviously a skilled and talented lover. Joanna became a compliant and demanding partner.

This was a wondrous new place for her, special and

beautiful. The controlled urgency of his need was a heady thing. It gave Joanna the sense that she had a certain primal power over this beautiful man.

He kissed, touched and tasted, until Joanna literally cried out for their joining. It was no longer an act; it was a need. She needed Gabe inside her to feel complete.

Poised above her, his brow glistening with perspiration, Gabe looked down at her with smoldering, heavy eyes. He waited for her to guide him, then filled her with one long, powerful thrust.

The sights and sounds around her became a blur as the knot in her stomach wound tighter with each passing minute, built fiercely until she felt the spasm of satisfaction begin to wrack her body. Gabe groaned against her ear as he joined her in release.

As her heart rate returned to normal, her mind was anything but. She lay there perfectly still, not sure what to do or say. She'd made love to Gabe with total and complete abandon. The experience was wild, primitive and scary. Her eyes fluttered in the darkness as she began to think of the consequences of her rash behavior.

"Where are you going?" Gabe complained when she slipped off the bed and wrapped herself in her slightly tattered robe.

"I'm just going to get a drink," she lied, careful to keep her back to him.

"Jo?"

Ignoring him, she all but ran from the room, needing space and privacy to try to understand her splintered emotions.

Joanna sought solace out on the balcony. The warm ocean breeze caught her hair.

"I thought it was the guy's job to run out afterward like a jerk," Gabe said as he came out and leaned against the railing. He hooked his thumbs through the belt loops of his jeans as he continued to stare at her.

"No postmortems, please?"

"Fine, then come back inside with me."

"I need to think."

"About what?"

Joanna met his eyes. "About why I just had unprotected sex with a man I don't know anything about. How's that for starters?"

She couldn't tell if the flash of anger in his eyes was because they hadn't taken precautions or if it was simply a response to her sarcastic tone.

"If it makes you feel better, I've never had unprotected sex before."

"Good," she acknowledged. "At least I won't die."

Gabe grabbed her by the shoulders and she realized it was taking all of his control for him to keep from shaking her.

"Are you worried about getting pregnant?"

She closed her eyes and drew in a deep breath. "Not until you just mentioned it."

"Then tell me why you can make love to me one

minute and stand on the balcony with a major chip on your shoulder the next."

"Because I don't do things like this," she returned hotly. "I live a very organized life with very specific goals."

"And I'm not one of them?" he thundered back.

"How can I possibly know that when I don't know anything about you?" she yelled.

"What the hell do you want to know?"

Joanna didn't have a ready answer. "I refuse to stand here trading insults with you," she announced as she tried to break away from him.

"Oh, no, you're not running off until this is settled."

"There's nothing to settle, Gabe. Let's just chalk it up to two lonely people who made a mistake."

"It wasn't a mistake."

Joanna rolled her eyes. "Really? Well then, if we were so ready to take this step, let me ask you a question."

"This is stupid."

"No," Joanna insisted. "I'm illustrating a point."

"But I'm not a jury, Jo. I'm not interested in hearing your closing arguments just yet."

"Fine, then answer one question for me. Just one."

"Okay," he said with a sigh.

"What's my favorite color?"

"That's a dumb question."

She looked up at him through her lashes. "It's not dumb. It shows how little we know about each other.

And just in case you think I'm attacking you, I'm not. I don't know your favorite color, either. I don't even know your middle name.''

Gabe's hands slid down her arms, gripping her just above her elbows. ''My favorite color is blue. My middle name is Brandon.''

''Too little too late,'' Joanna said as she jerked her arms free.

She turned and took one step, when Gabe grabbed her arm and said, ''There's something else you should know about me.''

Joanna didn't turn around. She simply spit out the word. ''What?''

''Rose Porter is my biological mother.''

Chapter Fourteen

"That's him," Joanna said with total confidence.

Detective Simms pulled the mug shot out of the binder and turned it over. "'Chuck O'Malley,'" he read. "Does the name mean anything to you?"

Joanna shook her head. "Sorry."

"We'll see if he's still at his last known address. If so, I'll need you to come back for a lineup."

"As long as it's before noon today," Gabe said.

The detective's brow wrinkled.

"I've got to get back to Charleston," Joanna explained. "I have a preliminary hearing that starts tomorrow."

After she promised to make herself available as soon as possible after the hearing, Joanna left the police station with Gabe in tow.

"Are you going to keep giving me the silent treatment?" Gabe asked as he started the car.

"I'm not giving you any treatment," Joanna replied as she kept her eyes forward. "We have just enough time to check out Joe Don and Shelia's place before our flight back.''

She refused to allow his hangdog expression or slumped shoulders to pierce her protective shell.

"I don't know why you're mad," Gabe persisted.

"I don't want to discuss it."

"Maybe I do."

"Maybe you should be discussing it with Rose."

"I had intended to," Gabe insisted. "I was working up my nerve, when Joe Don's demise intervened."

"And I'm supposed to believe you?" Joanna asked in a passionless tone. "Well, I don't know if I'll ever be able to believe anything that comes out of your mouth. You should have told me about your little masquerade."

"Why?"

Joanna made a disgusted sound. "Because it could have a bearing on the case."

"How?"

"Was Joe Don your father?"

"No."

"Then Harris can make a case that Joe Don somehow discovered who you were and confronted Rose with her secret, and she killed him to keep him from telling her sons."

"Aren't you grabbing at straws here?" Gabe countered. "There isn't even a remote possibility that Harris could know about me."

"I'm sure he's spent the past few weeks delving

into Rose's life. It is entirely possible that he discovered Rose had another child. Maybe she didn't kill him to keep her secret. Maybe Joe Don found out who you were and that you're loaded. Maybe he had plans to go after you for money.''

"You're forgetting one thing," Gabe said. "Either of your far-fetched theories would mean that Rose knows and has known for some time that I'm the baby she gave up thirty-seven years ago. I think that if she knew, she would have said something to me by now, don't you?''

Joanna shrugged. "Whatever."

"Want to know my theory?"

"Not particularly."

"I think you're using this to keep from admitting to me or to yourself that you feel something for me."

"Yeah, contempt."

"Don't you think you're being a little harsh?"

"You've been pretending to be something you aren't since I met you. I can't trust you. That's the bottom line.''

"We'll see about that," Gabe grumbled as he steered the car into the driveway of a sprawling single-story home.

Joanna kept her frigid exterior in place as she followed him around to the back of the house. It took Gabe less than a minute to pick the lock.

"Nice digs," he commented as they stepped inside the lavishly furnished home.

"Shelia has good taste," Joanna remarked as she

noted the custom-made furnishings and the decorator touches. "J.D. said his office was that way."

A large room at the front of the home had been converted into an office. They found filing cabinets—all empty—a computer—with its hard drive erased—and desk drawers with nothing but paper clips and dust balls.

"Someone was very thorough," Gabe said with a sigh.

"But they made one fatal mistake."

Joanna moved over to the desk and tapped the flashing red light of the answering machine. She pressed the Rewind button, then hit Play.

"This is Keith Winthrop. I've contacted my attorney and we're filing suit."

"He didn't sound like a happy customer," Gabe opined.

The next six calls were basically the same, give or take a few well-chosen expletives. "It seems Joe Don was in serious trouble," Joanna said. "I'm going to replay the tape and write down the names. I've got a friend from law school who has a practice in Palm Beach. Maybe he can run these for me."

"You do that. I'll be right back."

"Where are you going?" she asked Gabe, instantly sorry that the pang of fear in her voice gave her away.

He came and stood next to her. He started to reach for her face, but she flinched and backed away. There was a flash of sadness in his eyes, but she refused to let it affect her.

"I'll lock the door behind me. I'll be gone less than five minutes."

"Fine."

While Gabe was off doing heaven only knows what, Joanna got the names and called her friend. He promised to have what she needed within two days. He also suggested that Joanna authorize him to act as cocounsel so that he could subpoena Joe Don's bank records. Joanna readily agreed and thanked him for his time and his brilliant idea. If she was going to prove that Joe Don's murder had something to do with his business in Florida, she would have to present at least some evidence to the court.

"Hi, honey, I'm home," Gabe called as he came into the house.

"Not funny."

Gabe was grinning from ear to ear as he fanned himself with a small stack of mail. "I have something here that might interest you."

"So give it to me."

"Not until you promise to stop giving me the cold shoulder."

"I won't give you the cold shoulder," Joanna said as she made a grab for the letters.

"Tsk, tsk," Gabe teased. "Say it like you mean it."

"I mean it," she repeated flatly; then, forcing herself to smile, she added, "really."

Gabe dumped the stuff onto the desk.

"Tampering with mail is a federal offense," she said.

"Live dangerously, Jo," he prompted.

"I've done enough of that lately, wouldn't you say?"

"Ouch," Gabe teased her for the little dig. "Then I'll risk the federal rap to help you. Think of it as just a small example of what I'm willing to do for you."

"Stop it, Gabe."

"What I told you doesn't have to come between us," he said as he handed over half of the pile.

"It already has," she answered without the strength to meet his eyes.

Hating the pained tightness in her chest, Joanna thumbed through the thick envelopes. "With the exception of a few solicitations for credit cards or sweepstakes, most of these are from an attorney named Castle with an office in Miami."

"Do we open them?"

Joanna shook her head. "I'll call and see what I can find out."

"Well?" Gabe asked when she got off the phone nearly forty minutes later.

"It would seem that Joe Don absconded with his clients' escrow funds, leaving them with half-finished houses and no money in the bank. Mr. Castle said he was planning on having Joe Don arrested, as well as hitting him with a major civil suit."

"Does this help?"

Joanna shrugged. "It gives me the names of five

people I can suggest had a better motive than Rose did. Castle said he would contact his clients, and if they approved, he would fax me a copy of his files.''

"So where do we go from here?" he asked.

"Home."

LIKE SUSAN before her, Lucy mouthed the words "I'm sorry" as she passed the defense table on her way from the witness stand. It had been a pretty bad morning, as mornings go, and it wasn't yet eleven. Already Harris had called the medical examiner; the police officers who had investigated the murder; then Susan, who recited her tale about seeing Rose just before the body was discovered. Lucy had arrived looking like Lois Lane from the old television series, complete with brown wig.

"Why don't you ask some of these people questions?" Rose whispered harshly.

"Like what?" Joanna whispered back. "I don't have anything to challenge their testimony with."

"Then ask them if they think I'm capable of murder," Rose insisted.

"Irrelevant," Joanna answered before she placed her finger to her lips and gave her client a warning stare.

"The state calls Mitchell Fallon to the stand."

A rather seedy-looking man with a thin mustache and even thinner hair walked up to be sworn. His expensive suit wasn't enough to counterbalance the gaudy pinkie ring in the shape of a lion's head.

Don Harris stood, then broke from protocol by turning to Joanna and offering her a very satisfied smirk. She knew he wouldn't have done that if they'd had a jury present. Besides, Mitch Fallon was only going to say that Rose owed him money. He had told Joanna as much during their brief phone call the night before.

"Mr. Fallon, are you employed?" Harris asked.

"Yes."

"Doing what?"

"Objection," Joanna called out.

"Goes to foundation," Harris told the judge.

"Overruled."

Fallon seemed to squirm a bit before asking, "Our deal holds, right?"

"Side bar," Joanna screamed as she got to her feet.

Judge Adams nodded once and Joanna raced to the side of the polished wooden desk as she fought to keep her anger in check.

"What deal?" Joanna demanded of the smug prosecutor. "And why wasn't I made aware of any deals?"

"Calm down, Ms. Boudreaux. I'm sure Mr. Harris has a very good explanation for withholding information from the defense."

Harris didn't even flinch. He reached into the breast pocket of his suit jacket and pulled out a neatly folded document. "I have only the original of this, since Mr. Fallon just signed it a moment or two before entering the courthouse. His attorney, Greg Fletcher, is here

and was present when this was signed. If Ms. Boudreaux wishes, I'd be happy to put Mr. Fletcher on
the stand.''

"You did this on purpose," Joanna seethed.

Harris just grinned.

"Do you want a recess?" the judge asked. "I'd be
happy to give you an opportunity to review this agreement and question Mr. Fallon and his lawyer."

Joanna scanned the paper, then shook her head. A
recess wouldn't change the fact that Fallon had full
immunity from prosecution if he openly admitted to
loan-sharking.

"No." Joanna sighed. "But I would like the record
to reflect that Mr. Harris had several weeks in which
he could have offered this deal to Mr. Fallon and his
timing is, in my opinion, simply an attempt on his
part to circumvent the rules of discovery."

"So noted," the judge said. "Continue."

"Careful, Joanna, you're starting to sound a little
emotional."

"Burn in blazes, Harris," she answered between
clenched teeth.

Joanna took her seat next to Rose, who had gone
slightly pale. "What?" Joanna asked.

"Why is he testifying?"

"I don't know."

Harris straightened his tie and cleared his throat.
"Before Ms. Boudreaux panicked—"

"Objection!" Joanna yelled.

"That will be enough of that, Mr. Harris."

"I apologize to the court." Harris didn't sound all that sorry. "Before the—interruption—I asked you about your employment."

"I help people out," Fallon replied.

"How do you do that?" Harris asked.

"I lend them money."

"But you aren't a bank or an accredited financial institution, isn't that correct?"

"That would be correct."

"So you make unlawful loans?"

"Yeah."

"And did you make an unlawful loan to the defendant?"

"Yeah."

"And when was that?"

"About three and a half years ago."

"Did the defendant approach you about this loan?"

"Yeah."

"And did she ask you to do anything else for her?"

Fallon squirmed some more, and there was a sheen of perspiration on his forehead that set alarms off in Joanna's head.

"She was only making conversation," Fallon answered.

"Isn't it a fact that the defendant asked you how much you would charge to kill the deceased, Joseph Porter?"

Joanna closed her eyes as she heard Fallon answer yes.

Slowly Joanna got to her feet and said, "The defense would like a brief recess."

"Granted."

A few minutes later Joanna slammed the door and glared at her client. She was flanked by her sons, including Gabe.

"Don't you think it would have been a good idea for you to tell me about Fallon?"

"It wasn't like he made it out," Rose thundered in her own defense. "We were having a drink, and when I asked Mitch how he came to be a loan shark, he said it was because he had three ex-wives to support, and then I told him about Joe Don. We drank some more and then one of us said something like 'I'll kill yours if you kill mine,' but we were both a little drunk and it was nothing but talk."

Rolling her head around on her stiff shoulders, Joanna digested the information, then let out a long sigh. She met Rose's eyes and asked, "Is there anything else you haven't told me?"

Rose looked away. "No."

"One more lie and I'm out of here," Joanna warned. "I can't defend you if you can't tell the truth."

Joanna opened the door and found Dylan Tanner standing there.

"Tell me you found the French girlfriend?"

Dylan shook his head. "There were only three people and I've talked to all of them. No luck."

"Thanks," Joanna said with a small smile.

"Maybe you can talk to Rose and find out what else she's hiding."

"What makes you think she's hiding anything?" Dylan asked.

"The same way you probably know when your kids are lying. Just a feeling, and the fact that she won't make eye contact with me."

"I'll see what I can do," he said.

"Great. But court is back in session in ten minutes."

Joanna had every intention of taking those ten minutes to prepare her cross-examination of Fallon. She went back into the courtroom and took a legal pad from her briefcase, ignored Harris's cocky smile and retreated to an empty bench in the hallway.

She had written only a couple of questions, when she sensed him. "Go away, Gabe. I don't have much time."

"Don't take my head off."

She lifted her eyes to him. "Then go away. Or better still, go tell your mother that her failure to tell me the truth might just cause—"

Gabe grabbed her arm and gave her a little shake. "I didn't share that information with you so that you could announce it to the whole world."

"Why did you tell me?"

His expression was hard and unreadable. "You can figure it out. Fifth in your class, remember?" He dropped her arm. "I just came to deliver a message from Tammy. You've got a fax from that lawyer in

Miami and Detective Simms called and wants you to call back as soon as possible.''

"Thank you.''

"Don't mention it.''

Gabe stalked off and Joanna felt miserable. *Why am I so angry at him?* she asked herself for the umpteenth time. Well, soul-searching would have to wait. Her priority had to be her cross of Fallon.

Joanna managed to take most of the air out of Harris's balloon when she questioned Fallon. He told much the same story Rose had told, ending with the statement that "It was the liquor talking. I knew she wasn't serious.''

"The state calls Shelia Porter to the stand.''

Because of the gasps, Joanna turned to see what had everyone in such a dither. Shelia came into the courtroom dressed in black, complete with black handkerchief and veil. Lucy seemed to be studying her from her seat among the spectators, probably planning to add a grieving-widow persona to her vast collection of characters.

Aside from her name, Shelia didn't say much of anything on direct examination that could be called truthful. She even went so far as to claim that Joe Don had called her the afternoon before he died, begging her to take him back. Joanna had to pinch Rose twice to get her to stop going "humph!'' each time Shelia claimed to be heartbroken over the loss of her dear husband. She became so tearful at the end that she had flesh-colored smears all over her black hankie. It was quite a performance.

"Do you anticipate a lengthy cross?" the judge asked Joanna when Harris had finished.

"Yes, I do."

"Then we'll take our lunch recess now. Court will reconvene at 2 p.m."

"HOW'S IT GOING?" Tammy asked when Joanna and Gabe came in. "I had some deli sent over so the two of you could have lunch."

"Thanks," Joanna said.

"And don't forget to call Detective Simms. He said it was urgent." Tammy handed her the pink slip with the number on it.

"It isn't necessary for you to spend your lunch working," Joanna told Gabe when he followed her into the office.

"I don't really have anyplace else to go."

She met his eyes and felt her heart soften when she saw the dullness caused by pain and loneliness. "I guess I've been a little hard on you, huh?"

"Very hard," he corrected.

"I suppose there isn't really a decent excuse for the way I've treated you since…well, since…"

"We made love?"

Joanna heard Tammy drop her coffee mug and suddenly it was hard to keep a straight face. Her smile turned into a chuckle, then evolved into genuine laughter. Gabe joined her as he moved to take her into his arms. After the grueling morning, this was paradise.

"I've missed holding you," he said quietly as his fingers caressed the back of her neck.

"It's only been one day," she reminded him as she took a deep breath and allowed her face to rest against his solid chest.

"It seemed more like a lifetime."

"I know," she murmured.

"Have you figured out why I told you about Rose yet?"

"Don't make me think right now, Gabe, please?"

Tammy loudly cleared her throat. "I hate to interrupt, but Detective Simms said to make sure you called as soon as you got in from court."

Reluctantly, Joanna slipped out of Gabe's embrace and dialed the number. She listened intently, then braced herself against the desk before hanging up the phone.

"I don't believe it," she whispered.

"They caught O'Malley?"

Joanna met his gaze. "No. He wasn't at his last known address, so they looked in his record to see who his friends were."

"That's pretty standard," Gabe told her. "Felons usually hang out with other felons."

"Want to know who was with O'Malley when he was last arrested?"

"Joe Don?" Gabe guessed.

"Nope. Mitch Fallon, Rose's personal banker."

Chapter Fifteen

"Mrs. Porter," Joanna began in her most pleasant voice. "Do you know a young woman by the name of Maria Gomez?"

"I've met her," Shelia answered.

"Is she a friend of yours?"

"No."

"An acquaintance?"

"Not really."

"Was she your husband's mistress?"

Shelia reached under her veil and dabbed at her face, while her shoulders shook with sobs.

"Do you need a recess?" Joanna asked.

"No."

"No, you don't need a recess or no, she wasn't your husband's mistress."

"It didn't mean anything," Shelia sniffed. "Joseph's little indiscretions never meant anything to him. He always came back to me."

"Did he usually move to another state to have these indiscretions?"

"No."

"So, he left you nearly a year ago, but you testified that he called you the day before he died and begged you to take him back, is that correct?"

"He did," Shelia steadfastly insisted.

"Right," Joanna breathed as she walked back to the table and retrieved the list she had made during the lunch break. "Are you familiar with a Mr. and Mrs. Winthrop?"

"Yes."

"How about the Youngers, the Hiltons and the Fairfields?"

"Yes."

"Are these people all clients of the business jointly owned by you and Mr. Porter in Miami, Florida?"

"They were," Shelia answered. "We closed the business."

"You closed it?" Joanna repeated. "Isn't it a fact that all the people I just named have filed suit against the company you and your husband operated?"

"I think so."

"You think so or you know so?"

"I've gotten a few letters," Shelia grudgingly admitted. "Joseph was going to take care of those problems. It was just a bank error or something."

"Isn't it true that your husband was being investigated for embezzlement of client escrow funds? That he had been siphoning money from several people and leaving them with half-finished homes?"

"I don't know," Shelia wailed. "Joseph handled all the money. I don't know what happened."

"Isn't it also true that your husband was receiving threatening phone calls right up to the time he died?" Joanna asked.

"They were just angry because Joseph couldn't explain what he had done with the money."

"Nothing further," Joanna said. It was her turn to offer Harris a gloating smile.

Harris got to his feet for redirect with a computer printout in his hand. He had it marked, then gave it to Shelia. "Do you recognize this, Mrs. Porter?"

"This is a list of all the incoming calls to my home in Florida for the past six months."

"Will you turn to the third page, please? Approximately halfway down the page. Please read what it says for the court."

Shelia swallowed and then read, "March 5, 2:17 p.m., I received a call from Joseph's number here in Charleston. The call lasted a little over an hour."

Joanna closed her eyes.

"Nothing further," Harris said, sighing.

"Ms. Boudreaux?"

"Not at this time," Joanna said. "But the defense reserves the right to recall."

"Mrs. Porter, you have not been released by this court."

Shelia sniffed, smeared more makeup on her handkerchief and stepped from the witness stand.

"The state calls Peter Danforth."

"Why wouldn't he return my calls?" Joanna whispered to Rose.

"How the hell should I know?" Rose answered. "I don't even know this guy."

Peter Danforth, like his sister Michelle, fairly oozed money. It was apparent from his expensive clothes, his neatly trimmed hair, his buffed nails and his polished speech.

On direct examination, he explained that he had met the deceased through his sister, Michelle. That the deceased had called him with a business proposal and they had arranged to meet to discuss it.

"Was the deceased alone when this meeting took place?" Harris queried.

"No, he brought his wife along."

"Shelia Porter?"

Danforth shook his head. His hair didn't move. "No, he brought her. Rose Porter."

Joanna's stomach fell into her feet. She finally knew what Rose had been hiding all this time.

"He's lying!" Rose whispered. "I've never seen that man in my life!"

Joanna shushed her so she could hear Harris's questions.

"Did you subsequently come to some sort of agreement with the deceased and the defendant?"

Danforth nodded, but his hair still didn't move. "I agreed to loan them the operating capital for a new construction company. They convinced me that their plans to go into renovation were sound, and the defendant owned a successful business. The risks seemed minimal."

"I don't know what he's talking about!" Rose seethed.

Joanna shook her off again.

"And did you in fact give the deceased a check?"

"Yes," Danforth answered. "I gave him a check in the amount of three hundred fifty thousand dollars."

"And what, if anything, happened after that?"

"I learned that Porter had swindled a bunch of clients down in Florida. He had left more than a dozen jobs unfinished."

"What happened next?"

"I called Porter and told him I wanted my money back."

"What day was this?"

"March 1."

"Did the deceased return the money?"

Danforth shook his head. "He said he needed more time. That made me suspicious."

"Did you act on your suspicions?"

Danforth grunted. "You bet I did. I went to my bank to stop payment on the check."

"Was that successful?"

"Hell, no. Pardon me," he said to the judge. "Porter had put the money into his account, but it wasn't there when I had the bank run a check."

"How did you do that?"

"Porter and I use the same bank. The manager was

kind enough to check on the status of my money for me.''

''And what was the status?''

''The money was withdrawn the day after I gave it to Porter.''

''By the deceased?''

''By his wife, Rose. She's the one who signed the withdrawal slip.''

''I'M GOING to save the state the trouble and kill her myself,'' Joanna fumed as she stormed from the courthouse with Gabe right on her tail.

''I'm sure there's another explanation,'' Gabe insisted. ''She swears she didn't know anything about Danforth or the money.''

''Your judgment is understandably clouded,'' Joanna told him when they reached her car. ''You don't want to believe she's guilty—I understand that.''

His eyes narrowed. ''Don't patronize me. I'm simply asking you to think. If Rose took three hundred and fifty grand from Danforth, why didn't she write the check for your retainer?''

''Because she's obviously smart enough to know better than to dip into her little nest egg so soon after the murder.''

''Really?'' Gabe challenged. ''Then how come the merry widow is staying at the Omni?''

''Shelia?'' Joanna asked. ''But Danforth was very

clear that Rose was the woman with Joe Don when they met.''

''Maybe she was,'' Gabe conceded. ''But what if Joe Don told Shelia about his newfound wealth and she decided to help herself.''

''How?'' Joanna asked. ''And how did Shelia manage to be at the Rose Tattoo, killing Joe Don, when the DA gave me the names of five people who can swear Shelia was in Miami when the murder happened?''

''I don't have all the answers,'' Gabe said. ''I think we'd better go see Rose.''

Grudgingly, Joanna went with Gabe to the restaurant. They arrived to find that the place was closed to the public, but there was a somber crowd assembled. Rose and Shelby were there, as were Susan and Lucy, still wearing their court attire. Dylan was at the bar with J.D., Wesley and their wives.

Joanna yanked Gabe aside and pulled his head down to whisper in his ear. ''When are you going to tell Rose the truth?''

''When I think the time is right.''

''I feel uncomfortable knowing when she doesn't.''

''Sorry,'' Gabe said as he gave her a small squeeze. ''I'll tell her soon.''

Lucy was using a napkin to wipe away the theatrical makeup that had given her high cheekbones and a thinner, longer nose. Susan was clutching a crystal and chanting something indistinguishable. Rose was gulping down scotch.

"We didn't do very well today," Rose commented as Joanna reached the table.

"It might not have been so bad if you'd been straight with me from the start. I need to talk to you alone."

The two women glared at each other. Lucy stood, dragging Susan with her. In a perfect imitation of Judge Adams, she said, "We're adjourned. We should help Shelby out in the kitchen if we're going to get everybody fed."

As soon as the two employees left, Gabe came over. He gave Rose a hug before turning his seat backward and swinging his leg over the top. "Hang in there."

"Rose," Joanna began sternly. "I need to know everything, and I mean everything. I don't want to go back into court tomorrow and get blindsided."

"I don't know anything else," Rose insisted.

"Why is it that whenever you're professing innocence, you can't look me in the eye?"

Rose shrugged. "I didn't take Danforth's money. I didn't kill Joe Don." This time Rose said it while looking directly at Joanna.

"Okay. Here." Joanna folded the napkin that Lucy had used to remove some of her makeup. "Sign your name. I got a copy of the withdrawal slip from Harris and I'll see if I can find a handwriting expert who works nights."

Rose did as instructed. "It won't match," she said as she slipped the sample back to Joanna. "If I had taken the money, I would have paid Mitch the rest of what I owe him.''

''You haven't been paying regularly?'' Joanna asked.

Rose shook her head. ''I haven't had the cash. Mitch understood, though. I gave him free drinks when he dropped by. He floated the loan with no additional interest.''

''Did Mitch ever bring any of his friends here?'' Joanna asked.

''A few. I asked him not to because they seemed to bother the regulars.''

''How about a guy with a gold front tooth?'' Gabe asked.

''I remember him,'' Susan said as she came in carrying a tray of freshly cut vegetables and some dip. ''Remember him, Lucy? The guy had such a red aura I couldn't wait on him. You had to do it.''

Lucy shivered. ''How could I forget? I'll have the Cobb salad,'' she said in a voice that was very close to the one Joanna had heard in the garage. ''He tried to dress classy, but he still looked like slime—you could see it in his eyes.''

''He tried to kill me in Florida,'' Joanna told Rose.

''What?''

Joanna shook her head. ''It isn't worth rehashing, but it is rather strange that I get attacked and the guy just happens to be a friend of your buddy Fallon.''

Rose's green eyes grew wide. ''Do you actually think I would do anything to hurt you?''

It was Joanna's turn to shrug. "I only told you and my secretary where I was going."

"But we all knew," Dylan spoke up. "I came here looking for you when I had checked out Customs. There must have been a hundred people in this place when Rose told me where you had gone."

"ARE YOU SURE?" Joanna asked the wary-looking little man.

"I've signed your affidavit," he said. "The forgery was good, but not perfect."

Gabe picked her up and swung her around, kissing her hard on the lips as he did. "You're a brilliant lawyer," he told her as he reluctantly put her down.

"Fifth in my class," she reminded him with a wink.

"Maybe I should check out one through four."

"Suit yourself—they were all men."

They walked through the parking lot hand in hand. Gabe felt a real sense of contentment now that his relationship with Joanna was getting back on the right track. He began to think about taking her back to the beach with him. The memory of having her beneath him was permanently etched in his mind.

"Gabe?" She said his name almost demurely.

Good sign, he told himself. He wasn't going to have to think of an elaborate speech to get her to come home with him.

"Yes?"

"I want…" She faltered.

He stroked her arm with the back of his hand. "You want what?"

"I want you to go back to Miami."

"What?"

"I think Shelia is the murderer."

Gabe stopped and spun her so that he could see her face. "You actually believe Rose is innocent?"

Joanna gave him a small nod. "As you pointed out, Shelia is the one living at the Omni. I need to know everything about the business down there. Harris is going to call Michelle Danforth and Rose's landlady in the morning. If you take a flight tonight, you can get what we need and be back by early afternoon."

"And what are you going to do?"

"Miss you."

"WHERE'S GABE?" Rose asked when they met at their appointed place in the front of the courthouse.

"I sent him on an errand," Joanna answered. There was no point in getting Rose's hopes up just yet. "He'll be back by the noon break."

The rest of the Porter supporters began to arrive. Susan and Lucy came together; the Tanners and Rose's sons arrived just seconds later.

"We're losing a fortune," Rose complained. "Are you sure it's necessary for Shelby and the others to be here? We can't keep the Tattoo closed forever."

"It shouldn't be much longer," Joanna promised.

Before the judge took the bench, Joanna took a fortifying breath and went over to where Harris and his associate were seated. She placed her briefcase on the table, opened it, and handed him a copy of the handwriting expert's report. Then smiling sweetly, she said, "Have a nice day."

Michelle Danforth performed on the stand. She was so melodramatic that even the judge admonished her to confine her answers to what she actually saw or heard. Her testimony that Joe Don was afraid of what Rose might do if she discovered his infidelity was strong, but Joanna was able to neutralize it by getting Michelle to admit that to her knowledge, Rose had absolutely no inkling of what was going on. She also admitted that she didn't know whom Joe Don had asked to dress exotically. Joanna considered it a draw. Michelle didn't hurt them, but she wasn't exactly helpful, either.

"The state calls Mrs. Rupert."

A slender, mannish-looking woman with severely cropped silver hair took the witness stand.

Harris sauntered over to the railing, behind which a jury would normally sit, and leaned against it. Joanna rolled her eyes as he began speaking slowly, as if he were some bumpkin lawyer.

"Are you acquainted with the defendant?"

"She rents an apartment in the complex I manage."

"And how long has the defendant lived in that apartment?"

"Going on six years this August," the woman replied.

"And during those six years, have you had an occasion to talk with the defendant?"

"Of course."

"Would it be fair of me to say that you know the defendant's voice as well as her face?"

"Oh, yes."

"Were you at home on the night of March 5?"

"Yes."

"And where is your apartment relative to the apartment of the defendant?"

"I live downstairs from Rose."

Harris paused long enough to smile at Joanna. "And did something out of the ordinary happen on the evening of March 5?"

The woman nodded and the judge instructed her to respond verbally for the court reporter. "Yes."

"What happened?"

"Rose and Joe Don had a terrible fight."

"At about what time?"

"About eleven," she answered.

"And when you say it was terrible, what exactly do you mean?"

"Well...Rose chased Joe Don down the steps. She told him that if she ever saw him again, she'd kill him."

Chapter Sixteen

"You're just lucky I got the judge to grant a half-day recess," Joanna thundered at Rose.

"I understand that you're angry," Rose said. "I should have told you about that, but I never thought Enid was such a damned busybody."

Joanna paced back and forth on the carpet in front of the fireplace, completely oblivious to the fact that everyone was watching her outburst. "I can't keep asking for these recesses every time Harris knows something I should have known."

"Calm down. You have to think of your aura," Susan said as she brought Joanna a glass of iced tea. "Besides, we've all heard Rose and Joe Don go at it," she added. "They were always either yelling at each other or making up."

Lucy verified that point. "I've never seen people fight the way they did. It didn't mean anything."

"What were you fighting about?" Joanna asked Rose.

"He told me he had to go back to Miami."

"Then Shelia was telling the truth?" Joanna demanded.

"No." Rose, J.D. and Wesley all spoke as one voice.

"I know Joe Don talked to Shelia that day," Rose said. "He wasn't about to go back to her. He wouldn't tell me what they discussed, but I know he was furious with her."

"Then why did you threaten to kill him?" Joanna asked.

"Because I don't trust Shelia as far as I can throw her," Rose snorted. "She stole him once. I was afraid she would do it again."

"Do you know where he went after he left your apartment?" Joanna asked.

"I have no idea. He just said he had a business meeting."

"And an hour later he's here," Joanna stated. "What was he doing here? And how did he get in?"

"The place was locked," Rose insisted. "Joe Don and I had dinner. I know I locked the doors when we left."

"And they were locked when you came back?" Joanna asked Susan.

"Yes."

"Why did you come back?" Rose asked.

Susan blinked. "Because you told me to. Lucy and I both listened to your message on the machine."

"I did no such thing," Rose scoffed. "I think you need to get your crystals waxed. Why would I tell you to come back?"

"You told me to get the deposit ready," Susan insisted. "Didn't she, Lucy?"

Lucy nodded. "I heard the phone ring."

"I don't care what you heard. I didn't call you."

"Is there a reason for all this shouting?" Gabe asked as he came through the door carrying a bulging file case.

"It doesn't matter," Joanna answered. "Did you get everything?"

He nodded. "Probably more than you need, but I didn't want to have to make a second trip."

"What's all this?" Rose asked.

"Copies of all the building permits and bank records of Joe Don's construction firm in Florida for the past two years. We'd better take them to my office so we can spread them out," Joanna replied.

"Wait!" Rose yelled. "Aren't you going to stay here and get to the bottom of the phone-call thing?"

"If I'm right," Joanna said with a wink, "I already know who made the phone call."

"Who?" J.D. demanded.

"I'm not absolutely certain yet," Joanna hedged.

"Shelia?" Gabe guessed.

Joanna glared at him, but he only shrugged and said, "I looked through some of it on the plane."

"Don't any of you breathe a word of this until I have concrete proof."

"I always hated that woman," Rose said.

"LET ME GET another legal pad," Joanna said as she got up off the floor and stretched. They'd been going over records for hours and it felt as if they'd barely made a dent.

She reached into her briefcase and pulled out a pad, then stared at it for a minute. "Gabe!" she called. "I think you'd better come here."

"What?"

"Look at this pad."

He shrugged and said, "I'll go find another one."

"No!" she said excitedly. "Tell me what you think that looks like."

"It's smudged. As if you got putty on it."

"And forensics found what they mistakenly called putty on Joe Don's body and the desk."

"Where did you find it?"

Joanna went back into her briefcase and pulled out the napkin containing the handwriting sample they had gotten from Rose. Gingerly, she unfolded the crease and showed Gabe the makeup inside. "Oh, my God," she said as a terrible thought quelled her excitement.

"What?"

"Go to the land records," she insisted. "The homes that Joe Don was supposed to rehab or add on to. They're alphabetical, right?"

"Jo," Gabe said as he followed her into her office. "Where did you get the putty?"

"It's Lucy's theatrical makeup mixed with latex. If Lucy killed Joe Don because he cheated her, we all but announced that Shelia was as responsible as he was."

"What's her last name?" Gabe asked.

"McGuire."

"Oh, God."

"What?" she asked.

"There's an attachment to one of the foreclosures," he said as he dug through a stack on the floor. "Here it is."

"What is it?" As she watched his expression grow more concerned as he read the document, Joanna felt a deep sense of foreboding.

"Edward McGuire paid Joe Don almost five hundred thousand dollars to build his dream home in Palm Beach."

"Lucy's husband?" Joanna asked.

"This Edward McGuire was in his sixties, so I doubt it. See if you can find the contract or a copy of the canceled check."

"Why don't we just call him?" Joanna suggested. "It would be quicker."

"We can't. This says he committed suicide on the day the bank foreclosed on his property."

Joanna raked her hand through her hair. "What do we do?" she asked.

"Call Shelia?" he suggested.

Joanna went to the phone and, using her witness list, dialed the number to the Omni. She asked for Shelia's room, but got no answer.

"Should I alert the front desk?" Joanna asked.

"Alert them to what? With the way Lucy changes her appearance and voice, we couldn't even give them a decent description."

"Then what do we do?"

"We go to the Omni and wait for Shelia to come back. She's probably in the dining room having dinner or something."

"Or dead," Joanna whispered. "God, why did I even open my mouth?"

"I'm the one who said we were focusing on Shelia. If anyone is to blame, it's me."

"This is no time to be assessing blame. Let's go," Joanna insisted as she grabbed his arm.

"I think you should stay here," he said.

"I think you're wrong," she countered. "We can argue about it in the car."

They arrived at the Omni within a few minutes. Joanna had to jog to keep up with Gabe's long strides.

"Shouldn't we call the police or something?" Joanna suggested as they got off the elevator.

"Or something," Gabe answered as he knocked on the door of Shelia's suite.

"What if she's already dead?" Joanna whispered.

"Then you don't need to lower your voice," he said.

"This is no time for gallows humor."

"Sorry, a remnant from my days as a cop."

The door opened and Shelia, clad in a bathrobe with a towel around her head, glared at them. "What are you doing here?"

Gabe pushed inside, taking Joanna along with him.

"How dare you," Shelia huffed. "I'll call security and have the both of you arrested."

"Then you'll probably die."

Whether it was the tone in his voice that convinced

her or just the soft prediction, Joanna had no clue and didn't much care. The end result was that Shelia closed the door and meekly moved over to one of the two sofas that dominated the sitting room of the suite.

"What's this about dying?" she asked.

"Why don't you tell us about Edward McGuire?" Joanna countered.

Shelia blanched. "I don't know what you're talking about."

"Okay," Gabe said as he sat down and casually draped his arms on the back of the sofa opposite Shelia. "Then I'll tell you. Edward McGuire was an old guy who wanted to build his dream house. So Edward hires Porter Construction to design and build the house. How am I doing?"

Shelia's only response was a stony glare.

"Too early in the story to catch your interest?" Gabe taunted. "Edward takes his life savings and gives them to Porter, who puts them in an escrow account. Porter, as the general contractor, can withdraw funds whenever he needs to pay a subcontractor."

"I know my husband's business," Shelia hissed.

"I agree," Gabe said. "You knew it so well that you've spent the past two years skimming off a nice piece for yourself."

"You have no right to talk to me like this."

"Actually," Joanna said with a sigh, "you should be pleased we're only calling you a thief. A couple of hours ago, I thought you were a murderer."

"Jo, honey," Gabe said, "she *is* a murderer in the

strictest sense of the word. Aren't you forgetting Edward?''

Joanna nodded. "He's right, of course. Please accept my apologies. Do go on." Joanna sat beside him and smiled as Shelia's superior air seemed to evaporate.

"Edward discovers that Porter Construction has stolen all his money and he can't handle it. According to the papers, he puts a gun in his mouth and pulls the trigger."

Shelia closed her eyes and grimaced.

"Very messy," Gabe said. "And Edward's daughter was left to clean up the mess."

"This is where the part about you getting dead comes in," Joanna said.

"Edward's daughter follows Joe Don to Charleston. She has several advantages on him. See, Joe Don has this weakness when it comes to women…but you know that."

"I don't think I want to hear this," Shelia said.

"Sorry, but you will. Edward's daughter has a pretty easy time insinuating herself into Joe Don's life. She knew exactly what buttons to push. She was probably in the sack with him on the first night."

"I don't know what this has to do with me," Shelia protested.

"I'm getting to that part. Edward's daughter is not only attractive, she's kind of chameleonlike in her appearance. She can be a punk teenager or a graying old woman. A little makeup, a wig, the right clothes—"

"You forgot to mention that she's an actress and does a great Bette Davis," Joanna reminded him.

"Right. Edward's daughter hates Joe Don, and he's probably not thinking about anything above the belt. Edward's daughter also hates Rose, which, now that I think about it, gives the two of you a lot in common. Perhaps you'll end up at the same women's facility one day."

"You are not amusing me, Mr. Langston."

"Okay. Then I'll pick up the pace. Edward's daughter comes up with this elaborate plan to kill two birds with one stone—no pun intended. She can get rid of Joe Don and frame Rose for the murder. Lucy probably felt that Rose deserved to be punished for loving Joe Don all these years."

"Why are you telling me this?" Shelia asked. "Why don't you go to the police and have this daughter arrested?"

"Because the daughter isn't finished yet. She just learned that the real culprit, the person who actually took her father's money, the person who caused him to commit suicide, is you."

"I don't—"

Shelia's expected denial was cut off by the sound of someone knocking at the door.

"You might want to let me get that," Gabe said, all humor gone from his tone.

"I'll check the peephole," Shelia told him haughtily. "I have nothing to be afraid of. Certainly not a bunch of baseless accusations for which you have no proof."

As Shelia moved toward the door, Gabe stood and pulled a gun from inside his sock. "Stay back," he told Joanna.

"Don't worry," she answered.

"It's only that pathetic creature Rose," Shelia called. "Obviously you filled her empty head with this garbage, too."

"Don't!" Joanna yelled, but it was too late.

Gabe flattened himself against the wall, hidden just behind the opened door.

"Don't make a sound, Shelia. Just back into the room."

Joanna was wide-eyed. If she hadn't heard the voice, she would have sworn she was looking at Rose. Lucy had matched every detail, right down to green contact lenses and zebra earrings.

Lucy held a gun at waist height as she backed Shelia into the room. She hardly seemed to care that Joanna was there, as well. In fact, after the first moment of surprise, Lucy donned a smile of pure evil.

"Rose found her attorney with her hated rival and killed them both," Lucy said. "It works for me."

"But not for me," Gabe said as he came up behind her.

Lucy's smile faded, but just for an instant. She lifted the gun, took aim and fired.

Epilogue

"For someone who graduated fifth in her class, that was a very stupid thing to do," Gabe said as he walked into the hospital cubicle where Joanna sat on the edge of the bed while the nurse adjusted the sling.

"Reflex," she admitted. "I probably should have let Lucy kill Shelia."

"Are you okay?" Rose asked as she came barreling past one of the nurses. "I can't believe what Gabe told me tonight."

Joanna smiled at her client. "I'm sure he exaggerated. You should have heard him with Shelia. A little music and he'd make a great troubadour, with his gift for embellishment."

Rose beamed as she looped her arm through Gabe's. "Shelia stole my husband, then she stole his money." Rose chuckled. "I guess they both got what they deserved."

"Is Shelia in custody?" Joanna asked.

"Probably in a holding cell right next to Lucy," Gabe answered. "Don't expect her to send you a thank-you card for shoving her out of the line of fire,'' he added. ''She was so afraid I'd let Lucy have another crack at her that she went running to the police the minute they arrived.''

''It's all fuzzy,'' Joanna said.

''Probably thanks to that lump on your head. You hit the coffee table and blacked out when you tackled Shelia,'' Gabe supplied. ''She was almost twice your size,'' he teased. ''Not bad.''

''But tell her the best part,'' Rose urged.

''She already knows.''

Rose looked at Joanna with wide eyes. ''When did you tell her?''

Gabe actually blushed. ''When we were...in Florida.''

''You must think I'm a horrible person.'' Rose turned to Joanna. ''But I was only seventeen and—''

''I don't think you're a terrible person,'' Joanna assured her. ''In fact, you were just what I needed.''

''What?''

''I guess I'd gotten a tad jaded,'' she confessed. ''It was refreshing to work on behalf of someone who really didn't do it.''

''But Lucy was good enough that even I was starting to wonder,'' Rose said, laughing. ''Especially when Danforth insisted he'd met me, and Susan swore I had called her.''

''It's over now,'' Joanna said as she reached out with her good arm and squeezed Rose's hand. ''I'm sure they'll find that Lucy duplicated Susan's key. But the DA will only send you a form letter telling you how sorry he was to have put you to any inconvenience."

"Lord," Rose breathed. "That sounds like the same line they feed you when they don't have a sale item and they're trying to pawn off a rain check."

"You can sue him, but Harris really did have the evidence to support the charge."

"I'm going to take Rose home," Gabe said. "They told me you'd be at least another hour."

"Fine."

Rose came forward. "Thank you, Joanna."

"Just doing my job." Joanna smiled at Rose, but purposely avoided making eye contact with Gabe.

"C'mon, Gabe, we have a lot of catching up to do."

"I'll be back," he said as he lifted Joanna's hand to his mouth and brushed a kiss across her knuckles.

"Sure you will," Joanna said as soon as the curtain fluttered closed. "Well, Langston, I hate goodbyes, so I'll just save us both the trouble."

"Where are you going?" the nurse inquired as Joanna numbly got ready to leave the hospital.

"Back to my organized life with specific goals," she answered. She didn't bother to elaborate; she knew she would dissolve into tears if she tried.

"IT'S BEEN eleven days," Tammy said.

"Since what?" Joanna asked, glancing up from her desk.

"Since you ate or talked or laughed."

"I'm working on an appellate brief," Joanna answered. "It isn't all that amusing."

"You look like hell," Tammy persisted. "You must not be sleeping."

"Go type something, Tammy."

"You're doing everything, Joanna. By the time I get here in the morning, you've already done my work and yours."

"Then take a vacation," Joanna suggested, staring at the papers she was shuffling. "Take your kids someplace."

"I can't," Tammy said.

"Sure you can. You just jump in your car and go."

"But then there won't be anyone here to—"

Joanna looked up again. "You aren't making sense. I'll be here. I'm perfectly capable of answering the phone and opening the mail. I do it when you aren't here in the afternoons."

"Joanna?" Tammy said as she twisted her hair around her finger. "How mad would you get if I rearranged some of your schedule?"

"I don't care."

"But you always care," Tammy argued.

Joanna put down her pen. Her brow furrowed in confusion as she asked, "Is there something you want to tell me?"

"I...I think I'll go out for coffee," Tammy said.

"Good," Joanna murmured. "Drink slowly."

"You shouldn't treat her like that."

Joanna whipped up her head so fast that her hair fell free from its clip. "Gabe."

"How's your arm?"

"As good as new. How's Rose?"

"She's...Rose."

Joanna smiled and waged a silent war against the tears she felt pooling in the backs of her eyes.

"Thanks for stopping by," she said, lowering her gaze and trying to make it look as though she was hard at work.

"Have you figured it out yet?"

"Figured what out?" Joanna asked, then she cleared her throat and said, "I'm not pregnant, if that's what you're hinting around about."

"That's too bad, but Rose will be happy."

Joanna sucked in a breath. "You told Rose?"

"Yes."

"Why on earth would you tell her something so...private?"

"Maybe for the same reason I told you that she was my mother."

"You're talking in riddles," Joanna said.

"Riddles, huh? I guess that means I need to give you more clues."

"I have work to do," Joanna protested weakly.

"Here's clue number one," he said as he came around, lifted her out of her chair and gave her a bone-melting kiss.

When he finally released her, Joanna fell into her chair like a rag doll.

Gabe knelt before her and dug into his pocket. "Here's clue number two."

Don't read anything into it, she told herself. "What is it?"

"Open it."

"Oh, my gosh," Joanna breathed. "I don't know if I'll be able to raise my hand with a rock like this."

"Cute," Gabe said. "As the jeweler said, there is no such thing as a diamond that's too big."

"It's really beautiful, Gabe, but I'm—"

"Wait. Clue number three," he said as he reached behind him and pulled out an envelope.

"Plane tickets?"

"Yep, I thought it would be nice for you to see Paris in the spring."

"Very funny," Joanna said. "I can't go to Paris. I have responsibilities. I have work that needs—"

"The next clue," he said as he hunted down her purse and opened it. Smiling, he found her organizer, dropped it on the floor, then crushed it into a broken wad of plastic and wires. "It looks to me like you're free for the next month or so."

"Free to do what?" she asked.

"Get married, make babies, relax, let me pamper you."

"Sorry," Joanna said as she snapped the ring box closed and held it out toward him. "I can't, Gabe. I'm really sorry."

"I guess I'll have to give you the final clue," he said with a sigh. He caught her chin between his thumb and forefinger and tilted her face until their eyes met. "I love you, Jo."

She flew into his arms. "I love you, too. That should have been your first clue, by the way."

"Are you criticizing my proposal?"

"No, I'm accepting."

"Good."

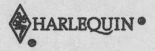

Heartbreak RANCH

Four generations of independent women...
Four heartwarming, romantic stories of the West...
Four incredible authors...

Fern Michaels
Jill Marie Landis
Dorsey Kelley
Chelley Kitzmiller

Saddle up with Heartbreak Ranch, an outstanding
Western collection that will take you on a whirlwind
trip through four generations and the exciting,
romantic adventures of four strong women who
have inherited the ranch from Bella Duprey,
famed Barbary Coast madam.

Available in March,
wherever Harlequin books are sold.

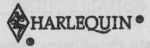

HARLEQUIN ®

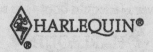

LOVE *or* MONEY?
Why not Love *and* Money!
After all, millionaires
need love, too!

**Suzanne Forster,
Muriel Jensen
and
Judith Arnold**

bring you three original stories
about finding that one-in-a million man!

Harlequin also brings you
a million-dollar sweepstakes—enter
for your chance to win a fortune!

 **HARLEQUIN** ®

HTMM

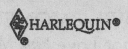
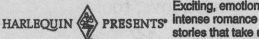

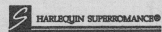